# ALASKA CHALLENGE

# ALASKA CHALLENGE

*By* Tom E. Clarke

LOTHROP, LEE & SHEPARD CO., INC.
*New York*

Library of Congress Catalog Card No: 59-13159



By American Book-Stratford Press, Inc.

Second Printing, October, 1960

# ALASKA CHALLENGE

# Alaska Challenge

BY TOM CLARKE

## CHAPTER I

"Well, Jerry," the officer said as he pulled the car marked Seattle Police over to the curb of the deserted, tree-lined street, "shall we let you out here or do you want us to deliver you right to the front door?"

"It makes no difference to me," Jerry Nelson mumbled sullenly from the back seat.

"But it might make a difference to your mother if she saw us bringing you home," the policeman said, "and it looks like she's waiting up for you." He nodded toward the lighted window gleaming out of the midnight darkness in the corner house half a block away.

"I'll get out here then." The tall, good-looking boy bent forward and reached for the door handle.

"Just a minute before you go, Jerry," the other officer sitting in front with the driver broke in. "I've a few things to say to you before you leave."

"Didn't Sergeant Dugan say about everything there was to say down at the station?"

"Well, he was pretty rough on you kids, all right, but you had it coming and if it had been for me to decide I might have jailed the whole bunch of you and not just Russ Wheeler."

"I don't see why they locked up Russ, even," Jerry said, brushing the unruly blond hair out of his blue eyes.

"You don't?"

"No, I don't."

"All I can say is you're mighty lucky that bird didn't pile into somebody when he was trying to get away from us and running all those red lights and dodging in and out of traffic at seventy miles an hour."

"Russ is a good driver."

"No one who pulls the stunts he did this evening is a good driver—just lucky," the officer snapped. "How do you think your mother would have felt if you'd had a smashup and someone down at City Hospital or the coroner's office would have had to call her up? With your dad flat on his back in the hospital since before Christmas because of a car accident you, of all people, should have sense enough to stay away from a wild kid like Russ Wheeler. How old are you, anyway, Jerry?"

"Almost eighteen."

"Almost eighteen—you're old enough to know better. You never used to get into trouble until your dad got laid up and your mother had to go to work. It's only since you've been on the loose and started running around with Russ and his crowd of hot-rodders—"

Jerry interrupted. "Well, *I* never did anything. I was just along for the ride and I can't help what the driver does."

"Any time you're with someone who commits a crime the law can hold you responsible, too."

"But, gosh, Mr. Elgin, a guy can't run out on his friends—that would be chicken."

"Then you should be a bit more careful about who you choose for friends."

Jerry was about to say that who his friends were was nobody's business but his own, but after the scene down at the station house he thought it best to remain silent.

"And there's something else I'd like to know," the policeman said. "Russ has never done an honest day's work in his life, yet he's always got gas for that jalopy of his and money for gadgets. What does he do, anyway—steal it?"

Jerry flared up. "Russ is no thief!"

"Oh? How do you know?"

"Well, I know I filled his gas tank tonight."

"You filled his gas tank. Well, all I can say is that buying gas for Russ Wheeler is like buying bullets for a crazy man with a machine gun. He's just as dangerous."

"Oh, you fellows don't like Russ because he's outsmarted you so many times," Jerry said, grinning. "Every time he turns around there's some cop waiting for him to make some little slip so you can pick him up."

"You bet your life we lay for Russ Wheeler," the officer said. "Our job is to catch guys like him when they first start showing signs of being trouble-makers and we try to straighten them out before they do something serious."

"Well, I don't care what you say, Mr. Elgin, I like Russ and I'm going to stick by him."

The two officers shook their heads slowly and sat in silence for a time. Finally the driver said, "All right, Jerry, if that's the way you feel about it go ahead and think that way, but I promise you one thing: if you must run around with Russ Wheeler then we'll be laying for you, too, even if your dad *is* Erik Nelson. Now that's a promise and don't forget it."

"I won't," Jerry said and his tone was a little more respectful. As he closed the door of the prowler car he heard one of the policemen reporting in to his headquarters by radio. Then the engine started, the lights came on, and the car pulled away and left him alone on the dark street. He started for home and as he walked slowly along, his sneakers making no sound at all on the sidewalk, he began wondering what he was going to tell his mother if she was waiting up for him. But maybe she'd be asleep. Then he could get out first thing in the morning and find something to replace the job he'd quit earlier in the evening so he could go off with Russ Wheeler and the gang.

But where would he find other work? The dishwashing job he'd left at Mr. Miller's drive-in café was the third he'd quit since school let out two weeks ago. It was already the middle of June and all the summer jobs in town were long since filled. He fingered the few coins he had left in his pocket from the twenty-three dollars Mr. Miller had paid him, and began wishing he hadn't been so hasty in quitting. After all, with his dad's hospital expenses and doctor bills and everything else, his mother *did* need the money. How would she feel when he told her that eighty cents was all he had left after filling Russ's gas tank and taking the bunch to the skating rink, then buying cigarettes, hamburgers and malts all around. That's the way it had been with the other jobs he'd had, too: Russ would show up where he was working and before the day was over he was out of work and broke. No, he wasn't looking forward to facing his mother at all. Not that she was going to say much . . . but she had a way of looking at him when he did something like this that —well, he just wished that he hadn't quit his job.

Except for the single light that was burning in the front room the rest of the house was dark. He hoped his mother was already asleep, but as he tiptoed up the back steps and into the kitchen he smelled tobacco smoke and heard the sound of voices. He walked quietly down the hall and hesitated in the doorway to the living room. His mother was seated on the davenport talking to a man who was smoking a pipe. Why, it was his uncle, Ed Carlson! What was he doing down here from Alaska? Jerry listened to what he was saying. "We sure didn't have time for any mischief like that when we were kids back in the old country."

"Things are different now, though, Edward. There is no more water to carry, no goats to milk, no wood to split, no clothes to scrub. Young people just have too much time on their hands these days."

Jerry coughed to make his presence known and as he entered the room his mother said, "Look who's here, son!"

"Hello, Jerry!" His uncle, a stocky, ruddy-faced

man, in his forties, got to his feet and came across the room to meet him.

"When did you get here, Uncle Ed?" Jerry asked as they shook hands heartily.

"Oh, about an hour ago. Say, you've really shot up into the air since I was down here last. Why, you're almost head and shoulders above me already." He turned to Jerry's mother. "Don't you ever feed this lad? He's nothing but skin and bone."

"He's just the way you used to be, Edward. He eats more than three stevedores right now," Jerry's mother laughed, and led the way to the kitchen.

"Oh, well, he'll fill out one of these days," her brother said, as he and Jerry sat down at the kitchen table.

"What are you doing down here from Alaska at this time of the year?" Jerry asked. "I thought this was your busy season."

"Any time of year is the busy season when you're slave to a gold claim," his uncle said, "but I've been wanting an excuse to fly down here to see for myself how your dad is getting along. So when my old truck gave out I figured this was the time to come Outside for a new one."

"How long are you going to be here?"

"If I can get hold of everything I need and load up tomorrow, I'll be heading North for the good old State of Alaska first thing the next morning."

"Golly," Jerry said, "that won't give you much time with us."

"I know, but by the looks of the pay dirt I was into when the freeze-up hit last fall I'm looking forward to my best year yet. And every day I'm away from the diggin's means just that much money out of my pocket."

"I sure wish you could stay longer."

"And so do I, but old Mother Nature won't stand around waiting for me to get there. When everything is just right I've got to be on the ground and ready to jump. Up to now the runoff from the snow melting back in the hills has made the Kasilof River too swift for freighting. But the water was dropping fast when I left and I've got to be on hand to start hauling my supplies up to Tustumena Lake as soon as the river is low enough."

Jerry's mother set a plate of sandwiches before him on the table. "I had a call from Mr. Miller at the drive-in tonight."

Jerry looked down at the toes of his shoes and nodded. "I suppose he told you I blew up and quit my job?"

"Yes." She brushed nervously at her apron. "Sergeant Dugan called, too."

"Well, those guys—"

"Was it true, son; what he told me about you and your friends?"

Jerry hesitated a moment before answering. "Yes."

She started to say something more but her voice broke and she hurriedly left the room. Jerry picked up a sandwich and bit into it savagely. But his mouth was dry, the food was tasteless and he couldn't swallow. Out of the corner of an eye he could see his uncle watching him intently. Finally Jerry put the sandwich back on the plate and mumbled, "I guess I'm not as hungry as I thought I was."

After a few moments his uncle said in a low tone, "Your mother tells me you've been giving her a bad time. Is that right?"

Jerry shrugged. "Oh, it hasn't been anything serious."

Ed Carlson cocked his graying head to one side and looked at Jerry through narrowed eyes. "Being picked up by the police sounds pretty serious to me."

"Oh, the cops are always laying for us guys."

"Then you must have been doing something. They don't go around arresting people for not doing anything."

"How do you know?" Jerry demanded.

"I've been in a few scrapes myself and the only times I've ever had trouble was when I got caught doing something wrong."

"Well, a guy is bound to make a little slip once in a while."

"Not if he watches his step he won't." Ed waited for his words to take effect, then his voice softened. "Three jobs in two weeks; that's no good, either, Jerry."

"I don't want to be a dishwasher all my life."

"A man has to start somewhere and the bottom is as good a place as any."

Jerry shrugged.

Ed pulled his chair up closer and laid his hand on Jerry's knee. "You're still pretty young and you've got plenty to learn and some smartness to be knocked out of you. But I've got a lot of confidence in you, Jerry, even if you have made a few mistakes."

"Thanks."

"Now I'm going to make you a proposition and you can take it or leave it—that's entirely up to you. Do you want to listen?"

"Shoot."

"I don't think there's anything wrong with you that a lot of good hard work won't cure. So how would you like to go up North and spend the summer helping out on my gold claim?"

## CHAPTER II

"Just what kind of work is it?" Jerry asked after considering the offer for a time. "What would I have to do?"

"Well, so you'll know just what you're getting into I'll tell you straight from the shoulder. The work is hard and there will be a lot of it and for the most part it will be the worst kind of drudgery there is—shoveling gravel into a sluice box. The days will be hot and dusty and the nights can get mighty cold, even in summertime. You'll get caught in wind and rain storms like nothing you ever saw in your life and there will be times when the gnats and mosquitoes will be so bad you'll think they're going to eat you alive. You'll have to wash and mend your own clothes and clean up after yourself and help with the cooking. There won't be any electricity, and if you want water you'll have to carry it from a stream in a bucket. Sometimes you'll be so worn out at the end of a day's work you'll go to bed wet and dirty and hungry and just be thankful you've got a dry spot to lie down on. It's a rough life, Jerry, but it's a man's life. My part of the country is still in pretty much of a primitive stage and the comforts are few. Now do you want to take a fling at it or do you think it might be too tough for you?"

Jerry looked up quickly. "What do you mean, too tough for me?"

"From what I hear about the way you've been carrying on lately, it makes me kind of wonder whether you've got what it takes."

"Maybe I don't want to go to Alaska. All my friends are down here."

"Maybe you need a change of friends as much as anything."

Once again the insinuation that his friends were no good angered Jerry, but this was no time to make an issue of it. He did like the idea of going to Alaska, though. "Do you really want me to go?" he asked after a time.

"Sure I want you to go, but as I said in the beginning, it's up to you and I'm not going to try to influence you one way or the other. I've told you about the tough end of the deal, now let me give you the other side of the picture. First of all, you'll see scenery and wild life you never dreamed existed, and you'll have experiences you wouldn't get in a lifetime of city living."

"And will I get paid for working?"

"Sure you'll be paid. You'll get a share of everything we take out of the ground."

"Well, how big a share?"

"That all depends on how much effort you put into it. The harder you work the more you can expect to get out of it—that is, if you stick it out until the freeze-up."

"And what if I don't stick?"

"If you're not planning on sticking then we'd better forget about the whole deal. There's no place up there for quitters."

"If I go I'll stick all right, don't worry about that."

"Good. Now mining is always a gamble and there's the chance the pay streak will run out and we won't make a dime. That's a risk we all take. But unless I miss my guess this is the year I'm going to strike it rich. All the signs point to it being even better than last year, and that was good. One thing's for sure, we get paid for what we do and the harder we work the bigger the stake will be at the end of the season."

"Well, that end of it sounds good," Jerry said.

Ed got a map from his suitcase and spread it out on the kitchen table. "Here is the Kenai Peninsula," he explained, "and this is our jumping-off place, Kasilof village, over here on the Cook Inlet side of the mountains." He put a calloused finger on the map. "We drive down here as far as Kasilof in the truck and go the rest of the way by river dory." He traced the course of the crooked river away from the inlet toward a range of mountains to the east. "Here's Tustumena Lake and way down here at the far end, 25 miles to be exact, is where my claim is located—right at the foot of Tustumena Glacier."

"Why there?"

"Because that's where the gold is."

"I know, but how did you happen to go to that particular spot in the first place; how did you know there was gold there?"

"Well, I didn't really discover it myself," Ed said. "I just picked up where the Russians left off."

"The Russians?"

"Yes. You see the first white men to settle in this part of Alaska were Russians who came over from Siberia hunting sea otter. Back in the 1700s and up until 1867 when the United States bought the country, all of these villages up here were Russian trading posts; Kenai, Kasilof, Ninilchik."

"And what about the gold?"

"When I first went North I lived at an Indian village on Cook Inlet. One day an old native came along and saw me prospecting in a creek. He told me that his grandfather, a full-blood Russian by the name of Simeanov, had been manager of a mine up at Tustumena Glacier back in the old days. I only half believed him but I wasn't doing any good where I was so I went up and took a look around. Sure enough I found some old ruins where he said they'd be. And there was enough gold sign about to make it worth my while to stake out claims and start washing gravel on the glacier flat."

Jerry's mother had come back into the kitchen and she frowned as she looked over their shoulders at the map. "But isn't it awfully dangerous, Edward, going through the rapids of that river, I mean, and with those big bears all around that I've heard you talk about? And there was that friend of yours who was so badly injured when the moose trampled him a few years ago . . . you know, the man who stayed here with us when he got out of the hospital."

"If Cliff Steele hadn't gotten careless, the moose would have left him alone."

"But it *is* dangerous up there?"

"Sure, it's dangerous. But so is getting out of bed in the morning if you aren't careful. Look what happened to Erik, and he's been driving cars for twenty-five years. Now I've run the Kasilof River over a thousand times since I've been in the North and I've killed at least a hundred brown bears—and nothing has ever happened to me. It's all in knowing what you're doing and how to do it. Jerry's a big lad and he's smart enough; he'll be able to take care of himself all right if he follows the rules."

"But he isn't eighteen yet."

"Now, look, Hilda, don't you remember before we all left the old country how Jerry's dad and I sailed in an open boat around the North Cape of Norway? And we weren't even sixteen then."

"But things were different in the old country."

"They weren't a bit different. It's just that you're his mother. Nobody knows how long Erik is going to be laid up; and if Jerry has to fill his dad's shoes and be the breadwinner, then he'd better start learning how to take the hard knocks when they come along. And besides, he'll be able to make ten times as much up there between now and freeze-up than he'd ever make here washing dishes and sweeping floors in some restaurant."

Ten times what he could make dishwashing! Jerry had no idea his earnings might be that much. This was beginning to sound interesting—and the mention of washing dishes and sweeping floors in a restaurant made it even more so.

"We *do* need the money," Jerry's mother admitted, "so I guess we don't have much choice. But I wish it wasn't so far away."

"Now Hilda, do you want him to go or don't you? I won't take him against your wishes—even if he wants to go."

Jerry's mother was thoughtful for a few minutes before answering. "I guess it is time he was making his own decisions. Do you want to go, son?"

Jerry sat looking down at the faded pattern on the linoleum, a pattern that was almost worn away from many years' usage. There were a lot of other things around the house that had outlived their usefulness, too, and should have been replaced had there been the money to do it with. Maybe this opportunity his uncle was offering him was just the chance he needed—and if he should strike it rich up North they could throw out the worn linoleum and paint the house, pay the medical bills and maybe he could even buy a car. Boy, a car of his own! It couldn't be too bad up there, he thought, despite what his uncle had told him. In fact he had always had a yen to see Alaska. Several of his schoolmates had gone North for the summer to work in the fisheries and he had envied them. His dad had been up there, too, and was always talking about the hunting and fishing . . . and that was something Jerry did like to do, hunt and fish. But would there be time for such activities or would it be a summer of hard work and nothing else? He asked about it.

"Why, sure you'll be able to hunt and fish," Ed said. "We don't work all the time up there—just most of the time." He laughed and went on. "We get all our meat off the country so you'll have to hunt and fish or else live on beans."

"Then I guess that settles it," Jerry said. "I'll take you up on your proposition."

"Good!" His uncle slapped him on the knee. "But there's just one more thing I want you to understand before we make it final."

"Yes?"

"I'm the boss up there. You'll have to do what I tell you—and the way I tell you to do it. Now you probably think I'm acting like a top sergeant when I say that, but in the North you've got to do everything right the first time. Too many things can go wrong when you're running white water or stalking a brown bear, and your first mistake might be your last. A greenhorn just can't go up there and do things the way he'd do them down here—everything is different. So when I tell you to do something you've got to do it and do it quick. Any argument with that?"

Jerry shook his head. "No argument at all."

"Do you still want to go?"

"Right," Jerry said. They shook hands on the deal.

Next morning at nine o'clock Jerry's uncle backed his new green truck against the loading dock of the Western Grocery Company warehouse near the waterfront in the lower part of Seattle. "I've got to go uptown on business for a couple of hours," he said as he shut the engine off and set the parking brake. "I want you to stay here and make sure that we get everything that's on the grocery order. Anything we miss is something we'll have to do without—or pay Anchorage prices for when we get up North. See that it's loaded as far forward as you can get it. Make sure the heavy stuff is on the bottom and put the light things on top. And before you start loading, be sure to take the tool box and spare tire off and put them on last so we can get at them in case of trouble. Do you think you can remember all that or shall I write it down?"

"Can do," Jerry said, making the O.K. sign with his thumb and forefinger.

"I'll go in and pay for the stuff now and when I get back we'll go down to the Acme Machinery Company and pick up the things they'll have for us there."

"Do you want me to meet you some place with the truck?"

"No, just stay here until I show up. I shouldn't be gone too long, but in case I'm not back by noon, here's some lunch money." Ed handed Jerry a dollar. Then after paying for the groceries he flagged a passing taxi and went uptown.

An hour later his uncle had still not returned and none of the supplies had yet appeared on the loading dock. Jerry went into the warehouse and found the shipping clerk. "How soon is the Carlson order going to be ready?"

"Gosh, I'm sorry," the man said, "but I had to put the whole crew to unloading a boxcar over at the other end of the building."

"When do you think it will be ready?"

The clerk looked at his watch. "We'll put a couple of men on it as soon as the car is empty. If you come back at eleven I think it will be ready to go."

Jerry went back to the loading dock. He was about to get into the cab of the truck when, a few blocks away over on the waterfront, a steamer whistled and began backing slowly away from its pier. Jerry crossed the busy road and started walking along the seawall. The air was filled with cries of seagulls, the chatter of cargo winches on moored ships, and the deep rumbling of diesel switch engines.

An unkempt, disheveled panhandler sidled up to him and said, "Could you spare a dime for a cup of coffee, buddy?" then hurried into a nearby tavern with the quarter Jerry gave him. Well, you learn something every day, he thought. The man *looked* hungry. A little further on he stood for a time at the window of a curio shop, then waited while a long line of traffic came rolling from the ferry slip just beyond. There was a brisk wind blowing in off Puget Sound. It carried the tang of salt and kelp and of the evergreen forests that grew on the far shore at the foot of the snowy Olympics, standing sharp and brilliant against the blue June sky. His uncle had spoken of the spectacular scenery that he could expect to see in the North but as he stood looking out across the sparkling green waters Jerry could not help thinking that here, in his own home town, was scenery spectacular enough in itself.

Yet he had never before thought much about it. He was so accustomed to his surroundings that he had always taken them for granted. Perhaps it was just because he was leaving it all that made him more conscious of the things about him. He felt a little strange inside as he thought about going away from his home, his parents, and everything else he knew so well. This would be his first experience away from home for any time at all and, for that matter, his first time away even from the State of Washington. His parents, who had come from Norway, half around the world, had always been content to stay right here in Seattle, once they were settled. But, unlike them, Jerry would never be content to stay in one place all his life.

Walking on he came to a dock where the odor of fish was heavy in the air. He stopped for a time to watch the crew of a deep-sea schooner unloading big, white-bellied halibut from the hold of their vessel, iced fish not long out of the deep North Pacific banks. A little further on a sleek, black-hulled steamer was being nudged gently into a slip by two tugs. As the ship inched in toward the shore Jerry could read the name, NAMBU MARU, and see the oriental characters painted immediately below. The vessel came to rest with its prow almost touching the seawall. Looking up, Jerry could see the overhanging forepeak where wiry little Japanese seamen peered out at the city and talked among themselves in their own tongue as they made the ship fast.

The wind brought the aroma of cooking and he followed his nose to an open-air dockside cafe. He bought a paper dish of fish and chips, crisp and brown, still hot from the cooking vat, then sat down on a bench under a gay-colored canopy on the pier. As he ate he watched the fireboats at the mooring near by, rising and falling gently in the swell. Jerry always enjoyed trips to the waterfront. He liked to think of the flow of commerce from all over the world that met here. And today he felt even closer to the hustle and bustle; for he, too, was now a part of all this, for wasn't he awaiting a load of cargo to help transport to a faraway place?

The thought jarred him! Awaiting a load of cargo to help transport—he looked at his watch. It was a quarter to twelve and he should have been back at the warehouse by eleven! Where had the time gone! Tossing the last of his lunch to a seagull perched on a nearby pilehead, he set off at a dogtrot toward the warehouse, muttering angrily to himself for having lost track of the time. He had a good mile to go, and when he got there the groceries would still have to be loaded. He wondered what his uncle would say if he came back and found he wasn't there. Plenty, he thought. His only hope was that Ed would be delayed himself and not get back. Then maybe the truck could still be loaded before he showed up.

It took him fifteen minutes to get back to the Western Grocery Company warehouse and when he arrived, out of breath from running, the shipping clerk met him at the door. "You're just in time," he said. "I was about to lock up and go to lunch." As the man spoke the noon whistles began blowing all along the waterfront. "We wondered what had become of you, young fellow."

"Oh, I got delayed up the street," Jerry said. "Is the stuff ready to be loaded?"

"I had a couple of boys sitting around with some time

on their hands so they loaded it up for you. Come on into the office and sign the invoices and you can take her away."

"Well, gee, thanks a lot." Jerry felt a great wave of relief. He reached eagerly for the sheaf of papers that the man handed to him. "Is everything all there?"

"I checked it on, myself."

Jerry signed his name to the papers and thanked the man again. He was just coming out the warehouse door when a taxi pulled up and his uncle got out. Whew, Jerry thought as he went down the steps, that was a close one!

Ed walked around the truck and pulled at the ropes that secured the stiff, new tarpaulin covering the load. "Say, that's a real professional looking job of loading and tying down," he said. "Where did you learn how to do that?"

"Well," Jerry said hesitantly, "you see I—I had some help from a couple of fellows that work here."

"I hope you thanked them for their trouble."

"I sure did."

"Well, we can't do anything more until after the lunch hour. What do you say we take a run up the waterfront and have some fish and chips at Ivar's?"

"Sure," Jerry said, "I can always eat fish and chips."

Jerry's mother was already there, standing by his father's bed when he and Ed Carlson walked into the hospital room that evening. His dad had always been an active man and it hurt Jerry to see him lying in the heavy cast with both legs elevated and held in traction by a system of weights and pulleys.

Ed walked over to the bed and the two men shook hands warmly. Then Mr. Nelson lay back weakly on his pillow. "Do you want to wrestle?" he asked, a feeble attempt at a joke.

"Well, at least I might have a chance of licking you for once," Ed said. They both laughed and Ed went on, "How are you feeling, Erik?"

"As if I'd fallen into a cement mixer!"

"How much longer will it be?"

"I asked the doctor about it today and he said in a couple of weeks he'd be able to take the cast off—maybe. It won't be too soon as far as I'm concerned."

Ed spoke again. "You'll be out of here turning handsprings before the summer is over, I'll bet."

"Well, maybe not quite that soon, but don't think I won't feel like it." Mr. Nelson turned to Jerry. "Your mother tells me you're going North with Ed."

Jerry nodded.

"I sure wish I was going along."

"And I wish you were, too, Dad."

"It's kind of a long way from home, though, isn't it?"

"Well, yes, but—well, I had to have a job, and—"

"What's the matter with your job at the drive-in?"

Jerry glanced quickly at his mother, then at his uncle, as he steeled himself for what he had to say. "Well, Dad, I guess you'll find out about it sooner or later, but I—well, I guess I've kind of gotten out of hand without you around to lay down the law."

"What do you mean, son?"

"I've quit three jobs since school let out and last night the police picked up a bunch of my friends for tearing around in a car and—well, I was with them."

Jerry's dad closed his eyes for a moment. After a time he looked up again and said, "That's something I hate to hear, Jerry, but as you say it's better that I get it from you than from somebody else. Has this got anything to do with your wanting to go off to Alaska—you aren't running away from a charge of any kind, are you?"

"No, sir."

"I'm glad to hear that because if you were, I'd have to forbid your going until you'd faced up to your responsibilities." He turned to Jerry's uncle. "Are you sure you want him to go, Ed, in spite of what he's just told me?"

"That's exactly why I want him to go," Ed said. "I don't think there's anything wrong with him that a summer of good, hard work won't cure. He's done nothing that's really bad—yet. And I never knew a kid that was worth his salt who didn't get out of hand once in a while."

"And I wouldn't give you a nickel for one that didn't," said Jerry's dad. He turned to Jerry again. "Gold mining is mighty hard work, son. Are you sure you can cut it?"

"Don't you want me to go, Dad?"

"A man hates to see his son leave home for the first time so I wouldn't be telling the truth if I said I did. But if you want to go North, then more power to you.

All I ask is that if you intend to be a miner then be a good one."

A nurse put her head in. "I'm sorry, but it's eight o'clock and all visitors have to leave now."

Jerry's father reached out and took his hand and gripped it for a moment. "I guess I won't be seeing you for a while, son. I could probably lie here and give you advice all night long, but I won't. Just listen to your Uncle Ed and do whatever he tells you. We grew up together and he's got a good head on his shoulders. He won't lead you amiss. And don't think he can't be one tough cookie when he has to." He turned to Ed. "And if he does get out of line, don't be afraid to show him who's the boss—you have my permission to do that." Then he added, "But I don't think you'll have to."

The two men shook hands, and Ed followed Jerry and his mother out of the hospital room.

Jerry hurried down the hall and pressed the elevator button.

## CHAPTER III

It was still dark the next morning and the stars were twinkling brightly in the clear sky when Jerry Nelson and his uncle finished breakfast and took their bags out to the truck. The birds that had roosted in the cherry tree in the back yard were awakening and starting to twitter. On the eastern skyline the jagged Cascade Mountains were sharply outlined by the brightening glow of approaching dawn.

Jerry had been anxious to get started but when he looked at his mother standing there alone under the corner street light he wished that he didn't have to say good-by. If his dad were home instead of lying up there in the hospital, it wouldn't be so bad, but leaving her alone like this—well, it made him feel all funny inside. Theirs was a closely-knit family and he'd been away from his parents only a few times in his life, and then it had only been for overnight or on a weekend. This was different, though; he was going to be 2,000 miles away and he wouldn't be seeing his parents for at least four months. But he was nearly eighteen years old, almost six feet tall, and on his way to Alaska to become a gold miner. And men didn't let their feelings get out of hand.

His uncle broke the silence. "I guess we'd better get rolling." He stepped over to Jerry's mother and gave her a brotherly hug and kiss and said, "Don't worry about the lad, Hilda, he's going to make out all right."

"I know he will." She came over and kissed Jerry and held him close to her for a moment. "Do be careful, son," she said. "We have all the faith in the world in you."

"Goodby, Mom, I—"

Ed reached over and put the truck keys in Jerry's hand. "You drive, don't you?"

"Sure."

"All right, then, wind her up."

Jerry jumped into the driver's seat and as soon as the engine came to life he tramped heavily on the throttle, sending sharp bursts of exhaust sound echoing down the deserted street. He had never before had the opportunity to drive a truck and the sense of its power excited him. He pumped the foot throttle again and his uncle jumped in beside him. "Go easy on that gas!" he said sternly. "What are you trying to do, wake up the whole town?"

"I'm just warming her up." Jerry eased off on the throttle.

"Not my truck you don't warm up that way," Ed said. "Let her run as slow as she'll idle until that temperature needle gets up to where it belongs. This is a brand new rig and I've got half a year's wages tied up in it. I want to get my money's worth out of her. Every time you goose a cold motor like that you do more damage to it than you would in a thousand miles on the road. Now don't you forget that or your driving days will be over as far as this truck is concerned."

"I'm sorry," Jerry said. "Nobody ever told me that."

"Well, you know now," Ed said. "Let her roll."

Jerry looked out the window at his mother and blew her a kiss, then put the gears into first range. As he let out on the clutch, the heavily-loaded truck started out with a lurch. His mother smiled and waved as they pulled away from the curb. Then Jerry swung around the corner and just missed a parked car, but they were on their way. He wished Russ and the gang could see him now!

The gears of the new truck ground stiffly as he shifted into second. He was about to change to high when his uncle said, "Pull over and stop!"

Jerry steered over to the curb, tramped down hard on the brake pedal and the truck came to an abrupt halt. Ed Carlson was thrown forward so hard he had to put out his hands to keep from banging his head on the windshield. "Holy Smoke!" he exclaimed angrily.

"What's the matter, did we forget something?" Jerry asked.

"You've just forgotten how to drive, is all," Ed said, "or did you ever know how?"

"Why, I've been driving for years."

"You'd never know it. Let me take that wheel."

"What's wrong with my driving?" Jerry asked, reluctant to give up his place at the controls.

"Just about everything. Who taught you?"

"Oh, a lot of guys."

"You sure picked up all their bad habits."

"Well, I'm not used to a truck—"

"All right, out of that seat. I'll take it while I still have a truck left."

Jerry's disappointment was bitter as he got out of the driver's seat and came around to the right side of the cab while his uncle slid over behind the wheel. "I thought I was going to get to do some of the driving," he said as he got in and closed the door.

"Not until you learn how."

"I'll never learn just sitting here."

"You'll get plenty of practice once we get out on the open road, but city streets are no place to practice driving a heavy truck, even this early in the morning. Do you know you almost hit a car when you came around that corner back there?"

"It's just that I'm not used to a truck, that's all."

"Knock off the alibis," Ed said, sharply. "Now I'm going to show you how I want it done." He started the engine. "I've already told you about warming the engine so we won't go through that again." He pushed in the clutch and put the truck into first gear. "There's no need to start out with a jerk the way you did. Give her quite a bit of gas and let your clutch in slow and easy—like this." The engine sound deepened as the throttle was advanced and the truck rolled smoothly away from the curbing. "And you don't have to grind your gears when you shift, either," Ed said, shifting quietly. They drove along in silence for some miles before he spoke again. "And anticipate your stops before you get to them, it saves on brake linings." He slowed the vehicle gradually and came to a gentle stop at a red blinker light.

While they waited for an early morning bus to go by, Ed said, "I think your big trouble back there was that you got in too big of a hurry." He looked up and down the street then said, "There isn't much traffic out here; do you want to give her another whirl?"

Jerry scrambled out and around, and got into the driver's seat again. "All right, what do I do?"

"Just take her slow and easy and you'll make out all right. Take it away!"

Jerry killed the engine starting out. "What did I do wrong that time?" he asked, stepping on the starter button.



"You took it a little *too* easy," his uncle said quietly. "Don't forget that you've got about three tons on the back end. Give her a little more juice this time."

Jerry waited for a car to pass, then speeded up the motor and pulled out into the intersection. His shifting of the gears was not as smooth as Ed's had been but there was no grinding this time. As they rolled out through the suburbs, he glanced over at his uncle and was given an approving nod that made him feel warm inside.

They headed northward toward Canada and four hours later had cleared Customs at the border and were bound for the Alaska Highway. Nightfall found them well up into British Columbia. When they stopped at a roadhouse for supper Jerry asked, "Are we going to spend the night here?"

"No, we'll go right straight on through since your driving has improved so much today. As soon as we've eaten, you can unroll your sleeping bag and catch a few hours' sleep. I'll wake you up at midnight and you can take her until daybreak."

Jerry had never realized how tired one could get from just riding and driving. The new truck rode hard, the roads had been bumpy, and he was more than glad to crawl into his sleeping bag atop the load. He lay for a time under the tarpaulin accustoming himself to the lurch and rumble of the truck and watching the lights of the cars they passed. How far had they come today, he wondered? Let's see, they had left home at four in the morning and it was past nine in the evening now. Except for brief stops for fuel and food and to trade places at the wheel they had been on the move constantly. They had been gone seventeen hours. Earlier in the day Uncle Ed had said that with the new truck and the mountains and the roads as they were, they would do well to average twenty miles an hour. That would place them a little over 300 miles from home.

Home! Jerry wondered what his mother was doing right now? Probably what she did every night—mending or cleaning, or perhaps out baby-sitting for one of the neighbors. He had never before given much thought to what his parents did when he wasn't around. His own evenings the last year or so had been full of one thing and another—shows, ball games, running around with the gang. He wondered what his friends were doing tonight. With Russ in jail, things would be pretty quiet. Russ was the leader and had all the ideas, and when he was around, things happened! Yes sir, he was going to miss old Russ, and he hoped his friend would get out of his trouble all right. In a way he felt himself to be just a little bit of a quitter for going off like this without trying to do anything for Russ. Then, in the midst of his many thoughts, he dropped off into a deep, sound sleep. He was disturbed only now and again by the flashing lights and roaring of an occasional vehicle that zoomed past going in the opposite direction.

It seemed as if he had hardly been asleep at all when a light was shining in his eyes and he felt someone shaking him. "Jerry, Jerry, wake up!"

Jerry lay for a moment trying to remember where he was. The truck was not moving and the engine was silent, but the roaring of the motor had not yet faded from his ears. He had the impression that they had just stopped. He tried to rub the sleep from his eyes and when he sat up his head came against the tarpaulin. "Oh, boy, am I worn out," he yawned. "Is it my turn to drive already?"

"No," his uncle said from out of the darkness behind the flashlight, "but we've got a flat tire. Where did you put the spare and the tool box?"

"The what?"

"The spare tire and the tools. Remember, I asked you to take them off before you loaded up and put them on last?"

Jerry came wide awake. "The spare tire and the tools? Why, I—" He sat thinking for a moment. The spare tire and the tool box; now what *had* he done with them? "Aren't they here on top of the load somewhere?"

"I can't find them," Ed said. "Are you sure you didn't leave them sitting on the loading dock at the grocery warehouse?"

A cold sweat came out all over Jerry as he recalled that when he had returned from his walk along the waterfront the truck had been already loaded and tied down.

"Think hard," his uncle said, "what did you do with them?"

"Well, I—they've got to be on here someplace."

"Did you put them on the load?" There was a tone of impatience in Ed's voice.

"I don't remember seeing them on the dock when we left."

"I asked you if you put them on. Now did you?"

"I don't remember doing it."

"Did you take them off the truck before it was loaded as I told you to; did you do that?"

"I don't remember."

Ed was silent for a moment then said crisply, "Now either that tire and the tools are underneath the load or else they are sitting on the dock back at Western Grocery—if they haven't been stolen by now. If they're under the groceries all we have to do is take everything off, but if we didn't bring them along—well, we're just out of luck."

"They must be under the load. They must have put the stuff on top of them while I was gone."

"While you were gone?"

Jerry realized he'd said the wrong thing.

"I thought you told me you were there when this truck was loaded?"

"I didn't say I was there."

"But you were supposed to be. Where were you, anyway?"

"Well, I—I took a little walk up the waterfront and when I got back the fellows had the truck all loaded."

"And you weren't there at all when they did it?"

"No, sir."

"And you don't know if the tire and tools are on or not?"

"No, sir."

"And you weren't on hand to check to see that all of our groceries were loaded, were you?"

"Well, the man said he checked them."

"In other words, you don't know what there is on this truck, do you?"

"No, but—"

Ed's voice rose in anger. "Blast it, Jerry, I left you there to see that we got what I paid for. Maybe we got everything and maybe we didn't. For all you know they might have just piled a lot of empty boxes on here."

Jerry remained silent.

"And I told you to see that the tire and tools were put on last, just so they would be handy if we did have a flat. You didn't do a thing I told you to do at all. You went for a walk down the waterfront instead!"

"They told me there was plenty of time—"

"I don't care what anybody else told you. *I* told you to check those groceries and to take care of the tire and tools. When you agreed to come North with me it was understood that I was to be the boss, right?"

"Yes, sir."

"And here we haven't been away a day yet and you've really got things fouled up proper. Now take that tarp off and get busy unloading. You're going to take every last thing off until you find that tire, and if it's not there you're the lad who's going to start walking to the next town for help. Now snap into it. I'm going to check the load against the invoices, and if we're short one can of beans it will come out of your pay at the end of the season."

Jerry wondered what kind of a deal he'd gotten himself into, anyway, being expected to pay for something he'd never even seen. Why, at that rate he could wind up the season owing everything he made and then some. And, after all, what was he to get in the first place—"a share of everything we take out of the ground," he had been told. That could mean anything—or nothing. What was it Russ Wheeler used to say? "Don't trust *anybody*." He wished he'd taken his friend's advice.

"I don't think I should have to unload the whole truck all by myself."

*"I'm* not going to do it," Ed said. "Now get busy. I'll hold the light for you and the quicker you get done the sooner we'll be on our way again."

"And what if I won't?"

"Then that will be the saddest day you ever lived, lad. I'll tell you one thing, Jerry. There's no way I can make you do it but I can sure make you wish you had. If I have to unload, then you're on your own and it's a long, long walk back to civilization. And people don't pick up hitchhikers along this road."

Jerry stepped over to the truck. "All right, you win." When the tarpaulin was removed he got back up onto the load and moved the machinery cases toward the rear. Then began the hot, back-breaking job of lifting each box and sack and carton out of its place. As each item came off, his uncle checked it against the invoices Jerry had signed so enthusiastically back at the warehouse. Two hours after he had begun, he came upon the spare tire way down on the bed of the truck. The tool box was right beside it.

He passed them down to his uncle, then climbed down and helped change the flat tire. When they were done Ed climbed up and finished his checking of the cargo. "Well," he said when he was done, "everything seems to be here except one sixty-pound keg of butter." He looked at the figures on the invoice under the flashlight beam. "And that will cost you thirty-six dollars—plus tax." Ed put the papers back into the glove compartment in the cab and handed the light to Jerry. "Here, you hold this for a while and I'll sweat for a change." He climbed up onto the truck and began tossing things back into place. Within half an hour they were reloaded, the tarpaulin was made fast and they were ready to go again. "Man, where did the night go?" Ed commented when he had the last knot tied.

Looking about him Jerry saw that the nearby woodland and the distant hills were beginning to take form in the gray light of early morning.

"Do you feel like driving for a bit?" Ed asked.

"I guess it's my turn, isn't it?"

"I'd say so, yes."

"I'll drive then." Jerry had never thought he'd see the time when he would be reluctant to drive but right now, more than anything, he wanted to go back to sleep.

As Ed started to climb up onto the load he laid a hand on Jerry's shoulder. "I'm sorry I blew my lid but if we had lost the tire and tools we'd really have been in a mess."

"Well, I guess I—"

"Let's forget it then," Ed said. "I've spoken my piece and as far as I'm concerned there's nothing to be sore about anymore."

*Maybe* we'll forget it, Jerry thought to himself. Aloud he said, "I was pretty sore myself."

Ed climbed up on top of the load, then said, "But don't let it happen again or you'll be on your way home on the first airplane."

"I won't," Jerry promised. He got into the cab and headed northward.

He did a lot of thinking as he drove wearily along the dusty, crooked highway. A lot of things were beginning to crop up about this whole deal that he wasn't liking at all. He had never had much trouble with his folks when it came to having things his own way. But this uncle of his—wasn't he just a bit too strict, too hard-boiled to have to put up with for a whole summer? Just about one more blow-up like the one they'd just had and he was through—deal or no deal and uncle or not. He had heard there were plenty of good-paying jobs in the North for anyone who wanted to work and once they hit Alaska—well, he was open for anything. If Ed Carlson wanted some character he could push around he'd just have to find himself another boy. Jerry Nelson was about fed up with the whole set-up!

## CHAPTER IV

Taking turns at the wheel, Jerry and Ed drove around the clock, stopping only to fuel and service the truck and to eat. The route took them through dense forests and over dreary prairies; they crossed barren muskeg country and followed deep gorges through spectacular, towering mountains. They were heading ever northward into the land-of-no-night-at-all where at this time of year at midnight the reds of each sunset blended with the pinks of the dawn that followed. They passed through frontier towns whose names had found their place in the history of the North—Dawson Creek, Fort Nelson, Whitehorse. It was at Whitehorse that Ed pulled the truck off to the side of the road and pointed to a long line of abandoned sternwheel steamboats tied up along a riverbank. "There's the Yukon, Jerry. This is where the stampeders passed through on their way to the Klondike in '98." He took out his pipe and filled and lighted it.

"You mean back in the Gold Rush days?" Jerry asked.

"That's right. Those were the *real* days and there's times I kind of wish I'd been born fifty years sooner.

Anvil went through it all and I envy him his experiences."

"Anvil?"

"Anvil Bergen, an old-timer who shares my cabin and has some claims adjoining mine up at Tustumena Lake. He's one of the last of the sourdoughs." Ed put his pipe away, then started the truck. As he headed down the road he shouted the lines of "The Shooting of Dan McGrew" loudly enough to be heard above the roar of the engine.

They crossed the border into the State of Alaska early the next morning and twenty-four hours later, after six days on the road, they pulled into Anchorage. Ed brought the truck to a stop, they got out and he put a coin in the parking meter.

"Parking meters in Alaska?" Jerry exclaimed as he stretched the knots out of his road-weary legs.

"You didn't think we were so uncivilized that we wouldn't even have parking meters, did you?"

"After all those miles of empty country we just came through I thought there'd at least be a place to park when we got here."

Ed brushed the dust from his clothes. "I've got some business to take care of at the Land Office, Jerry, and it will probably take me a couple of hours. You can look around a bit if you want to, but don't get too far from the truck. When I get back we'll pick up some stove oil and gasoline, then head for the Kenai Peninsula."

When his uncle had gone Jerry stood leaning against a fender of the truck for a time looking about him with interest. The sprawling young city showed signs of having grown too fast. Although the main street was paved, a fine white dust lay upon everything and the mud on the shoes of almost everyone who passed was evidence of back streets not yet surfaced. He had always thought of Alaska as being a land of ice and snow and fur-clad natives. But the day was hot and clear and the only snow in sight was on the tops of distant mountains. And so far he had not yet seen anyone who might have been an Eskimo.

There was something about the place that was entirely different from anything Jerry had ever known, but he couldn't put his finger on it. Everyone seemed to be going someplace in a hurry and he was impressed by all the bustle that went on about him—the buses, trucks and taxis rolling by and the steady stream of aircraft passing over, heading into and out of nearby air fields. Alaska was not quite what he had expected. But he was not at all disappointed. Something about the country quickened his pulse, made him breathe more deeply and he felt as if he wanted to start doing things.

Jerry was anxious to get to the claim and begin digging for gold. He had given up the idea of backing out of the deal he had made with his uncle. After all, Ed Carlson really wasn't such a bad guy once you got to know him. True, he wouldn't stand for any foolishness. But by watching his step and doing everything the way it was supposed to be done, there had been no more run-ins since the trouble over the tire and the keg of butter. On the long trip up the highway Jerry had had a lot of time to think over the incident and at last he had admitted to himself that it had been his fault. Lack of a spare tire out on the open highway was a lot different than being without one in town. He didn't blame his uncle for being sore about it and sometime, when the opportunity came up, he was going to tell him so.

Jerry crossed the street to a drug store and bought picture postal cards. He addressed them to his parents, adding a note telling of their arrival in Anchorage. He was just dropping the cards into a letter box when he heard the sound of music in the next block. Drawn by the sound he walked on down the street. A missionary stood in front of a barroom strumming a battered guitar. Next to him, a woman played an accordion while they both sang a vigorous revivalists' hymn in shrill, high-pitched tones. A pale little girl in a shabby dress and scuffed shoes handed him a religious tract and shook a tambourine in front of him. "Something for the Lord, please, sir?"

Jerry was feeling in his pockets for a coin when he became aware of loud voices coming from within the saloon. Then the double doors popped open and two unshaven young men in rough clothing propelled by a bald-headed man wearing a white apron came flying out onto the sidewalk. "If you guys gotta fight then do it out on the street!" he bellowed, then went back inside. The drunks took a swing or two at each other, then shook hands and went arm in arm into another bar.

"One guy's scared and the other is glad of it," a voice at Jerry's elbow said.

"It sure looks like it," he answered, turning toward the speaker, a fellow of about his own age.

"Why, Jerry Nelson!" the other exclaimed.

"Well, if it isn't Al Henderson!" Jerry grinned as he recognized an old classmate from Ballard High.

"When did you come North?" Al asked as they shook hands.

"We just drove in a little while ago."

"What are you doing up here?"

"I'm on my way to the Kenai Peninsula. My uncle has a gold mine down there."

"Well, good for you, Jerry," Al said. "How long are you going to be in town?"

"As soon as my uncle finishes his business in the Land Office we're going to leave. What are you doing here?"

"I'm working on a cannery tender."

"Doing what?"

"Deckhand."

"Here at Anchorage?"

"No, the cannery is on the Kenai River; that's about seventy miles or so down Cook Inlet from here."

"How far is that from Kasilof?"

"Kasilof is just beyond Kenai. Are you going there?"

"That's our jumping-off place," Jerry said.

"Maybe we'll get to see each other now and then."

"Well, I don't know. Where we're going is up a river and way down at the end of a big lake somewhere up near the mountains."

"Oh, that would be Tustumena Lake," Al said. "If that's where you're going, we won't be seeing much of each other."

"What are you doing now—today?" Jerry asked.

"I'm on my way back to the boat. We came up here to get some supplies for the cannery and we're supposed to leave as soon as the tide begins to ebb." He glanced at his watch. "Jumping Jupiter, I should have been back there an hour ago! Well, it's been nice seeing you, Jerry, but I've got to run. If I'm not there at sailing time the skipper will go off without me. And that will mean good-by job." Al felt in his pockets. "And I don't even have enough money left for cab fare."

"I'd like to help you, Al, but I'm about broke myself."

"Did you say you just drove in?"

"Yes."

"Have you got a car or something?"

"My uncle's truck is up in the next block."

"I wonder if you could take me down to the boat?"

"Where do you have to go?" Jerry asked.

"She's tied up down at the Ocean Dock."

"Where is that?"

Al pointed toward Cook Inlet. "Just down over the hill and across the railroad tracks."

"How far is it?"

"No more than a couple of miles," Al said.

"Well, I've got the keys and Uncle Ed won't be back yet for a while." Jerry thought for a moment. "I suppose I could take you down and get back before he does."

"I don't want you to get into any trouble, Jerry."

"Oh, I think it'll be all right."

"Well, that's sure swell of you."

"Come on, let's go then." They climbed into the truck, and ten minutes later Jerry parked at the end of the Ocean Dock not far from where a black-hulled tugboat was moored.

Al jumped out. "Lucky for me she hasn't sailed yet. Why don't you come aboard for a minute, Jerry?"

Jerry looked at the time. "I'd like to but I'd better be getting back uptown."

"The skipper won't be so hard on me for being late if you go aboard with me. How about it, Jerry, just for a minute, huh?"

"Well—all right, but just for a minute." Jerry followed Al to the perpendicular ladder that led down the face of the dock to the SUNSET, a cannery tender. Looking down, Jerry could see the muddy water boiling out from beneath the dock. The vessel's lines were drawn taut by the current of the ebbing tide. "Boy, that water sure is swift," he commented.

"The tide here drops thirty feet in less than six hours," Al said, starting down the ladder, "so it has to go out fast. The only place in the world where the tides are any higher than here on Cook Inlet is the Bay of Fundy, in Nova Scotia."

Jerry followed his friend down the wet and slippery ladder. When they were aboard the tender Al stuck his head into the pilot house and called, "About ready to go, Skipper?"

The burly, middle-aged captain came out on deck. "Where you been, anyway?" he demanded. "We've got to move up the dock and take on a few rolls of webbing and then get out of here before the tide drops too low. Where's Dick?"

"We went uptown together but I haven't seen him for a couple of hours."

"Who's your friend here?"

Al introduced Jerry to the captain. "Do you want a job?" the man asked. "As of right now we're in need of a new deckhand." He added for Al's benefit, "And if you'd been five minutes later we'd have needed two."

"Well, thanks a lot," Jerry said, "but I've got a pretty good job lined up already."

The captain looked up and down the dock for a moment, then said, "If that bird doesn't get here pretty quick we'll lose the tide and have to lay over till tomorrow. We can't let the lines go with only one deckhand when the current is running like this."

"Maybe Jerry could help out, Skipper," Al suggested.

"Did you ever handle lines before?" the captain asked.

"I've been on boats down on Puget Sound," Jerry said. "If I can help out I'd sure be glad to."

"Good." The captain was reassured. "I'll let the spring line go myself and Al will take care of the bow. Now you get back there on the fantail and when I give a blast on the whistle you unbend those turns off the bitt and then we'll move up a hundred yards. When I blast again you toss the eye around a piling and make her fast. Got it?"

"Aye, aye, sir!" Jerry said as the captain disappeared into the pilot house. Fantail? He assumed that must be the back end of the boat. He went there. Unbend the turns off the bitt—now what did that mean, anyway? It had to have something to do with untying the boat from the dock. He walked over to a rope that led out through a hole in the vessel's side, went around a piling of the dock, then came back inboard and was wrapped around a mooring bitt. That must be it; take the line off so the boat would be free.

The captain stepped out of the pilot house for a moment to unfasten a line and then went back inside. From deep within the hull of the vessel Jerry heard the clang of a bell. A puff of black smoke shot from the stack, the engine coughed to life and as the deck began to tremble underfoot he heard the sharp, quick toot of the whistle. Up forward he saw Al cast off the bow line. Let's see, unbend the turns off the bitt. As Jerry reached for the heavy rope wrapped around the bitt, the prow of the SUNSET began to swing out away from the dock. The rope was heavy and stiff and clumsy to handle and already the momentum of the boat had drawn it too tight to loosen. Caught by the boiling current of the ebbing tide, the tug pivoted so that it hung with its stern still fastened to the piling, its bow pointing at right angles straight out from the dock. The bell clanged again and as the engine began to run full speed in reverse, the straining propeller churned the water under the stern to a brown froth.

"Cut her loose!" the captain bellowed from the pilot house. Al came running down the deck, drawing his sheath knife as he came. Pushing Jerry aside he slashed at the taut, creaking rope. The hawser parted with a snap and the tender surged away from the pier, borne by the rushing current. The captain put the helm hard over and the bow began to come around—but not quickly enough. Moments after she had been cut free, the sixty-five foot vessel rammed hard aground on a mud bank a hundred yards way from the dock. The bell clanged again, the engine died, and the water stopped boiling out astern. The captain came storming out of the pilot house, cursing loudly, his face red with anger. "Why didn't you cast off when I blew the whistle?" he demanded, striding up to Jerry.

"I tried to—but everything happened too fast."

"I should have known better than to ask a greenhorn to cast off for me. I thought you said you'd been on boats?"

"Well, they weren't very big."

"Rowboats, I suppose?"

Jerry nodded. "How am I going to get back to the dock?" he asked when the captain's rage had subsided a bit.

"Well," the man said icily, "it looks like you're going to have to do like the rest of us—wait till the tide comes in again and floats us off this mud bank."

"How long will that be?"

"If we're lucky we'll be afloat in eight hours—maybe ten."

"But I've *got* to get back." Jerry sounded desperate. "My uncle will be coming out of the Land Office any time now and if he finds me gone he'll tear me apart." He looked up at the small boat suspended from davits atop the deckhouse. "How about putting me ashore in that?"

The captain looked over the rail at the current, then shook his head. "We've got no motor for it and you could never buck the current with a pair of oars. You'd wind up somewhere down around Kalgin Island if you tried that."

In the few minutes that passed since they had gone aground, the tide had dropped until they could see mud on all sides of the tender. "Maybe I could walk ashore," Jerry suggested.

"You'd go into that goo up to your neck if you tried it," the captain warned. "It's too thin to walk on and too thick to swim in. Your only chance of getting off this tub before high water is to grow yourself a pair of wings and fly ashore—and you don't look like no angel to me."

"What can I do then, anyway?"

"I don't care what you do. As for me I'm going to catch myself some bunk time and think about what kind of an excuse I'm going to give the cannery superintendent for putting his boat on the bottom."

When the captain had gone to his cabin and slammed the door shut behind him, Jerry sat down on the hatch beside Al and contemplated his fingernails for a time. "I must be a jinx," he said.

"What makes you say that, Jerry?" his friend asked.

"It seems like I just can't do anything right; everything I do goes haywire."

"Oh, don't take it so hard," Al said, laying a hand on

Jerry's shoulder. "It's really my fault you got into this pickle."

Jerry shook his head slowly. "No, Al, my uncle won't see it that way. I was supposed to stay and watch the truck."

"You're watching it," Al said, indicating the truck parked on the dock a hundred yards away across the channel.

"Sure, I'm watching it, all right, but what could I do if some guy came along and got in and drove off?" He felt in one pocket and then another. "Oh, man, and on top of it all I left the key in the ignition. My goose is really going to be cooked when Uncle Ed comes out of the Land Office." He thought the situation over for a time. "And if anything happens to that truck or the load then I might just as well keep on going."

"That uncle of yours must be a demon," Al said. "I never knew you to be scared of anybody or anything."

Jerry thought for a moment before answering. "He's really all right but he won't stand for any monkey business."

"Well, what can he do to you that's so awful? You're too big to lick. About all he could do is bawl you out good and that never hurt anybody."

"Oh, I'm not scared of what he might say or do to me. I guess I'm really scared of what he's going to think when he finds out I've let him down again."

"Oh, well, everybody makes mistakes."

"But I've made too many, Al. What I'm scared of more than anything else is that he'll put me on the first airplane for home. And I don't want to go. I've given my folks enough trouble already and if I can't even hang onto a job working for my own uncle then I guess I'm a flop."

"Here, maybe a smoke will make you feel better," Al said, taking out a pack of cigarettes.

Jerry shook his head. "I don't like the taste of them."

Al lighted a cigarette and pitched the match overside into the mud. When he had put the pack away he said, "I don't know, Jerry, but the skipper might still let you take Dick's place."

"Not after running his boat aground, I'll bet he wouldn't."

"Oh, he's not so bad once you get to know him. His bark is worse than his bite. Want to go ask him?"

"Not now," Jerry said. "I want to think this thing over some more. I'm going to have to face the music sometime so I guess the quicker I get it over with the better."

"Well, there's nothing we can do until the tide comes in," Al said, "so I'm going below and get a little shut-eye. There's a spare bunk in the fo'c'sle if you want to join me."

"No, I think I'll stay out here and see if I can figure this thing out."

"Well, suit yourself." Al disappeared down the companionway hatch into the dimness of the forecastle.

Just what *am* I going to do, Jerry thought as he sat looking across the channel at the truck, so near but yet so far. As the captain had said, about the only way to get off this boat right now was to sprout wings. He wondered what Russ Wheeler would do if *he* were stuck here like this. Of course, Russ wouldn't give a hoot whether he got off or not—but if he *had* to he'd figure out a way, somehow—you could be sure of that. Like that time last winter when they had gone for a drive into the mountains. A blizzard had come up and had gotten stalled in the snow. Jerry had thought that they were done for. But good old Russ had gotten them out of that one by tearing the wooden floorboards out of his old car and tying them to their feet like snowshoes. They were able to walk out to safety, and his folks had never been the wiser. Now he would never have thought of that himself.

Snowshoes! Say, why wouldn't that work here, too? Why wouldn't a couple of boards fastened to his feet keep him from sinking into the mud? It wasn't much more than a hundred feet to the solid beach down there at the head end of the channel. That was the ticket, boards on his feet! Good old Russ, to the rescue again.

Jerry looked about the deck. Boards and rope were all he needed. Well, here were boards, lying right on top of the hatch; a bit long and just a little on the narrow side, perhaps, but they should keep him from sinking into the mud. Rope? There was a coil of it hanging in the rigging.

Jerry took out his pocket knife and cut two lengths off the coil. The best idea, he thought, would be to tie the boards onto his feet first, then lower himself over the side of the boat. He went up to the bow and tossed the loose end of the mooring line over, then sat down on the bulwark and tied the boards on. Nothing fancy, but it should do the trick and that was all that mattered.

He had a little trouble getting over the side of the SUNSET with the eight-foot-long slats tied to his shoes. But once he had both feet outboard there was nothing to it, and he quickly let himself down the dangling mooring line. Jerry tested his weight on the boards and when he saw that he wasn't going to sink in, he let go of the line, and stood for a moment to make sure of his balance. Then he took a step forward. Nothing to it! He took another step away from the boat and was on his own. He had to keep going now because there could be no turning back. But why turn back; this was a cinch.

Ahead of him the mud sloped steeply down into the water to his left, and to the right, the bank flattened out on top. The boards wanted to slide down the slope and he thought he had better move up onto the level before heading for the beach. The boards were too long to do a skier's herringbone up the slope. He lifted his right foot and set it higher on the bank, then picked up the left foot and placed it where the right one had been. Now what did his skiing friends call that maneuver—the side-step, wasn't it?

He lifted his right foot again, then the left. Just a few more of these side-steps and he would be on top of the bank. Right foot up, left foot up, right foot—oops! Say, that mud is slippery, isn't it? Just like trying to walk across so much grease. Have to be more careful. Right foot, left foot—oops, watch it, there! Darn that slick stuff.

Right foot, left—woops! He tried to pick his left foot up before the right was solidly in place—hold everything! He started to slip sideways, down the slope. His improvised snowshoes were trying to act like skis and he wished he had a set of poles, something to stop his slipping. He leaned in toward the bank to try to stop the slide. In an effort to brake himself he clutched at the cold, slimy mud with his right hand but he slipped faster and faster down the bank, and left a furrow of long fingermarks trailing behind.

Jerry glanced quickly over his left shoulder. If he didn't stop and stop quickly, in about five seconds he would be in the channel and in that current with the boards tied to his feet he wouldn't have a chance. Why didn't I stay on the boat, he thought in a moment of panic. In desperation he threw his weight toward the bank and the next moment sprawled face down in the mud, legs tangled up in the boards. But he wasn't sliding any more.

Jerry tried to push himself up out of the mud but his arms went to the elbows into the smelly, sticky mess. "Al!" he called out desperately. "Hey, Al, give me a hand!"

A moment later Al Henderson's head appeared at the top of the boat's companionway hatch and he looked around. "What's the matter, Jerry? Where are you, anyway?"

"Down here!"

Al's mouth dropped open when he saw Jerry lying in the mud a short distance off the port bow of the stranded tender. Al looked as though he couldn't believe what he was seeing. "Don't tell me you tried to jump ashore," he called down to Jerry. "Boy, you sure didn't get much distance, did you?" He began to laugh.

"Never mind how I got here," Jerry yelled. "Get me out!"

Al laughed again.

"It isn't funny!"

"If you could see yourself you'd laugh, too," Al howled. "Oh, if I only had a camera!"

The captain came out of the pilot house, looked down at Jerry, then grinned. "Well, I'll be—" he said after a moment. "You're a persistent cuss, aren't you?"

Jerry struggled to get to his feet but his efforts only made him slip downhill toward the water again.

"Don't move!" the captain ordered. "I'll toss you a line!" He got a rope and threw it out so that it fell across Jerry. "Bend a turn or two around you and we'll hoist you aboard!"

Jerry got the rope under his arms and made a knot; then the captain and Al began hauling in, dragging him through the mud, up the side of the vessel and onto the deck.

"Just what in the world were you trying to do, anyway?" the captain demanded when Jerry was aboard. "What are those boards on your feet for?"

"I thought they'd keep me from sinking in so I could get ashore."

The captain looked at the boards. "Those are my hatch battens! And where did you get that rope they're tied on with?"

Jerry indicated the coil of rope in the rigging. "I cut it off of there."

"We've got a hundred fathom of worn-out rope back

there on the fantail and you cut up a brand new heaving line."

"I'm sorry." Jerry began working at the slimy knots that held the boards to his feet.

"Forget it," the captain said, "rope's cheap. Take him below, Al, and help get him cleaned up. Then I want every last speck of mud scrubbed off this deck."

When the captain had gone back to his cabin Al laughed again. "Yes, sir, Jerry, I'd sure like to have a picture of you right now."

"Oh, knock it off, Al, knock it off."

The mud had soaked through to Jerry's skin and when he had gotten his clothes off Al said, "You better go below and take a shower. I'll put your duds to soaking. And go easy on the water because we don't carry much aboard."

Jerry went down the companionway ladder and found the tiny shower room in one corner of the forecastle. He was mad at Al for laughing at him, mad at himself for getting into the mess, and mostly mad at Russ Wheeler for putting the idea into his head. Yes, it seemed as though every time he went along with one of Russ's ideas he got into some kind of trouble—even if he was 2,000 miles away.

Jerry was just about to step under the shower when he saw his reflection in a mirror fastened to the bulkhead. He looked at himself for a moment then began to chuckle. No wonder Al and the captain had laughed. He was really a sight!

## CHAPTER V

"Hey, Jerry!"

Jerry had just finished his bath and was getting into a pair of Al's dungarees when his friend called down to him from the deck. "What do you want, Al?"

"The truck is gone!"

"What?" Jerry hurried up the companionway.

"The truck isn't on the dock anymore."

"Where did it go?"

"I don't know. I was busy trying to wash the mud out of your clothes and I happened to look up and it was gone."

"Man, oh, man!" Jerry looked out across the mud flats and the narrow, deep-water channel toward the dock. "She sure is gone."

"What do you suppose happened to it?"

"Probably stolen," Jerry said. "I'll bet I've seen the last of that truck and everything on it."

"What are you going to do now?"

Jerry sat down heavily on the bulwark and stared out across the inlet toward the snow-crowned range of peaks to the west. "Guess my best bet would be to take to those mountains and become a hermit," he said woefully. "I'll never be able to face Uncle Ed now."

What *was* he going to do, Jerry thought? His best bet, he figured, was to get away from Anchorage and go some place else as fast as he could. Maybe Ed would have cooled off by the time they met again. He wondered about getting the deckhand's job that was open here on the boat. "What do you think, Al?" he asked after a time. "Do you suppose the captain really would give me a chance at that job, after everything I've done?"

"He's in the galley right now. Why don't you ask him?"

"He's liable to throw me overboard if I do."

"Oh, he's not that tough. Come on, it won't hurt to give it a try."

The captain was leaning against a bulkhead with a cup of coffee in a tattooed hand and staring off down the inlet. He turned as the boys came into the galley.

"Are you busy, Skipper?" Al asked.

"What's on your mind?"

"Go ahead and ask him," Al whispered hoarsely to Jerry.

"Say, Captain," Jerry began, hesitantly, "are you still sore at me?"

The captain eyed him carefully and emptied his cup before answering. "Forget about it, Slim, it wasn't your fault at all. I'm sorry I flipped my lid and bawled you out."

"Well, I was wondering—do you still need a deckhand?"

"I thought you said you had a good job lined up?"

"I did, but—well, I don't think I have now."

"That truck, huh? Is that the trouble?"

"Yes."

The captain looked Jerry over carefully again. "You're big enough and you should be able to handle the job if you're not afraid of work."

"Oh, I'm not afraid of work."

"Dick wasn't either. He could lie down right alongside of it and go sound asleep," the skipper said with a twinkle in his eye. Then he added, "By the way, are you eighteen?"

"Well—why, sure," Jerry fibbed.

"Good. You have to be eighteen before I can hire you. Have you got a social security card?"

"It's in my pocket."

"Then you've got yourself a job. The bookkeeper will fix up the papers when we get to Kenai. How about a cup of coffee and a bite to eat? I don't want any hungry mouths in my crew."

Jerry was about to answer when Al took hold of his arm and pointed out the open galley door. "Say, look what's coming down the road. Isn't that your uncle's truck now?"

Jerry watched the green truck with the tarpaulin-covered load coming down the road with a cloud of dust boiling out behind. "By golly, that's it, all right!" he exclaimed. As he watched, the truck came to a stop on the dock and someone got out. "And there's Uncle Ed!" he said with elation in his voice.

Stepping out onto the deck of the boat he cupped his hands and shouted, "Hey, Uncle Ed! Ed Carlson!" As the figure beside the truck looked around Jerry waved his arms wildly and shouted, "Hey, Uncle Ed, I'm out here on the boat!"

He could see his uncle shade his eyes with a hand to ward off the afternoon sun, then heard him call, "What are you doing there?"

"We're aground!"

"I can see that!"

"I can't get off until the tide comes in!"

He saw Ed look at his watch. "I'll be back for you at high water!" he shouted. He climbed back into the truck and headed up the road toward Anchorage.

"Well, at least, now we know the truck wasn't stolen," Al commented.

"Boy, and lucky for me it wasn't!" Jerry wondered then about the job he had accepted. It had been his intention to just leave on the tender and say nothing. But things looked different now. Perhaps it would be better to wait and see how he stood with his uncle before he did anything else. After all, he had no one to blame for his predicament but himself, and he couldn't just go running off without so much as a word of explanation. Yes, he had better stick around and face his responsibilities. That's what his dad would want him to do, and that was the least he could do to repay his uncle for the trip North.

He finished washing his clothes and hung them in the rigging to dry. Then he got a bucket of water and a brush and began to scrub away the mud that he'd brought on deck.

The racing current of the Cook Inlet tide lifted the boat off the mud bank shortly after six o'clock, and a few minutes later they were moored to the dock again.

"Aren't you going to sail with us?" the captain called after Jerry as he started up the dock ladder.

"I want to talk to my uncle first," he called back.

When Jerry came up over the top of the ladder Ed Carlson was waiting with angry eyes and a jutting jaw. "You'd better have some pretty good answers or you're in for a quick trip home," he said. "Now start talking and tell me how you got fouled up so good this time."

"Well, you told me not to get out of sight of the truck—and I didn't."

"No, you just left it—with the keys in it—and got yourself stuck out on a mud bank where you could keep a real good eye on it! Go ahead, how did it happen?"

"Honest, Uncle Ed, I didn't get more than half a block from the Land Office when I ran into Al Henderson, a kid I used to know in school. He was late and was afraid he'd lose his job if he didn't get back to the boat right away so I brought him down."

"Why didn't you come right back instead of going for a boat ride?"

"The other deckhand didn't show up and they had to move the boat and the captain asked me to help with the lines. I was a little bit slow and we wound up out there in the mud."

Ed nodded. "It's easy enough to do. Anything else?"

Jerry shook his head. "That's all there was to it. I'd sure have gotten back if I could have."

"Well, you gave me a scare, all right. When I came out of the Land Office and found you gone I went to the police station. The cops are on the lookout for you right now. One of them found the truck here and brought me down. We couldn't figure out if the truck had been stolen or what; and, well, I kind of thought you might have fallen off the dock and been carried away by the tide. Believe me, I was worried there for a while."

"I suppose I'd better get my stuff together and—"

Ed looked down into the tide rips swirling past the dock then laid a hand on Jerry's shoulder. "No, just climb into the rig and we'll be on our way to Kasilof."

"Aren't you going to send me home then?"

Ed shook his head. "If you had gone off joy-riding I sure would have sent you home, but since you were just trying to help somebody out, well . . . Now climb in there and let's get rolling. I loaded the gas and stove oil while I was waiting for the tide to come in, so we can head straight for the Kenai country."

"I'm sure sorry I've caused you so much trouble."

"Skip it."

Jerry went to the edge of the dock and called down, "I won't be going with you, Captain. Thanks a lot, anyway."

"What did you mean by that?" Ed asked as they got into the truck.

"Well, I had a job lined up, if you'd fired me. I didn't intend to go home. After all, I did come up here to make some money."

It was ten o'clock in the evening and the sun had just gone down behind the Aleutian Range when Ed turned off the highway. He drove down a road that wound through the woods and stopped in a small clearing beside the Kasilof River. "This is my winter place," he said as he got out of the truck and led the way to a cabin of square-hewn logs. He stood on the bank looking out at the stream for a time. "The water looks just about right for a good trip," he said. "Let's go turn in and get a few hours' sleep in a real bed for a change. We'll launch the boat and get her loaded first thing in the morning."

Jerry was watching the milky water slip quietly by, gurgling now and then as it swirled around the roots of trees that came down, it seemed, to dangle their feet in the gentle current of the Kasilof. "Is this the river that's supposed to be so swift and dangerous?" he asked.

"This is it."

"It looks pretty tame to me."

"Well, it isn't. Just listen! Do you hear that?"

Out of the forested distance upstream, a hollow roaring sound could be heard. "What is it?" he asked. "What's making all that noise?"

"Oh, that's just the river coming down Silver Salmon Rapids," Ed said.

"It—it sounds like a waterfall."

"And you'll think it is, too, first time you see it."

"Do you mean we'll be going through where all that noise is coming from?"

Ed nodded and indicated the stream flowing silently past. "This is the tidal river down here. The tide backs up for about another mile above here, and beyond that she's white water all the way to Tustumena Lake—seventeen miles of it."

Jerry listened to the roaring sound for a moment then said, "Is—is this trip necessary?"

"If you're going with me, it is." There was no hesitation in Uncle Ed's voice. "Well, come on, let's go in and catch a couple of hours of sleep. We've got a long day ahead of us tomorrow."

The cabin was filled with the aroma of fresh, hot coffee and frying bacon when Ed jerked the blankets off Jerry in the morning. "Up and at 'em," he said. "Breakfast is on the table."

Hurrying into his clothes, Jerry went out into the crisp outdoors. He washed in cold water from a bucket that stood on a stand beside the door. The sun had not yet risen but it was full daylight even though his watch said it was only three o'clock.

When they had finished eating and the dishes were washed and put away, Ed led Jerry to the launching ways on the river bank. "We've got to get the boat in the water first of all," he said.

Jerry looked at the stream. "I'd swear that river was running the other way last night."

"It was." Ed started turning the crank on the hand winch that lowered the boat down over the bank. "The tide is coming in now and she'll give us a lift up to Haystack Rapids."

They slid the big, white-painted open river dory down into the water, then loaded groceries, gasoline and stove oil aboard and covered everything with a canvas tarpaulin. "We'll take the machinery and the rest of the stuff up another time," Ed said. He threw a pair of oars on top of the load, clamped the two new heavy-duty outboard motors to the stern of the boat, and filled the gasoline tanks. "Now, Jerry," he said, adjusting the controls of the motors, "if you'll give us a shove out from the bank, we'll be on our way." Jerry pushed the boat out into the river then jumped aboard and found a place in the bow where he could sit facing forward. There was a roar, as first one and then the other motor came to life. The boat surged ahead.

For the first mile the channel was drowned by the incoming tide that pushed in from Cook Inlet, making the Kasilof flow backwards, against itself. Aided by the tidal current, they made good time, passing cabins here and there on either bank. Settlers came out to watch and wave a friendly hand as they went past. When they reached the upper limits of tidewater the smoothness of the river ended and as they entered the first series of rapids, the stream became boisterous and noisy. The motor sounds deepened as the engines began laboring to breast the heavy boat against the foaming current.

For a time Ed steered in close to shore, and they had to duck their heads to miss the drooping limbs of trees that stood upon the bank. Then they ran the middle of the channel for a while, skirting sunken rocks and hidden bars. The Kasilof was a crooked river, twisting right and left, in sweeping loops but leading always upward through the forest lands and toward the mountains.

They passed under the steel highway bridge and

some distance beyond, they went to the bank to refuel. When they stepped ashore for a moment to stretch their legs, Ed looked at Jerry's shaking hands. "Scared?"

Jerry nodded and shouted back so as to be heard over the roar of the river, "This is more than I bargained for!"

His uncle grinned. "Good! As long as you stay scared you'll respect this old stream and won't go taking any chances!" He pointed to an overgrown path that ran along the river bank. "That's the old Russian boat trail over there. You want to feel lucky we've got motors to do the work for us—those old-timers hauled their boats up here with ropes!"

"How much more of this rough stuff do we have?"

"Silver Salmon Rapids is just ahead and that's the worst part of the river. Once we're past there, we've got her licked. We should be at Slackwater in two more hours."

"It won't be too soon to suit me."

"Let's get going then." Ed got back into the boat, and Jerry shoved off from the bank and jumped aboard. As the motors came to life, they moved slowly past a boulder where a gray-winged gull perched and watched them going by. Staying in close to the right bank where the current ran less rapidly, the boat moved on. Around a bend the treetops opened up and Jerry was awed by the torrent that plunged down at them. A series of low waterfalls, one stacked above the other, reached upward and away as far as he could see, with a spray spun by the boiling waters hanging over all.

How could the boat get past this roaring barrier? And if it did, how could it keep from being slammed against the rocks and upset, or else be torn apart? How could a person, if thrown into the water, survive long enough to reach the shore? If I'm going to die, then I'm going to die, Jerry thought, and there's nothing I can do. But how are Mom and Dad going to feel about it? He got to thinking then about his folks and made up his mind that should the boat be upset, he must somehow get to shore alive. If this river tried to drown him, then it was going to have to put up an awful fight!

While he pondered the immediate future, Ed steered in between two rocks and found another opening just beyond. He cut across the stream to the other side and then came back again, further up the channel. He skirted by a bobbing tree trunk that had toppled from the bank and, lying crosswise to the current, clutched at them with naked limbs as they went past. Now and again, the morning sun reflected momentarily from the glistening sides of leaping fish, and Jerry knew why they called this Silver Salmon Rapids.

Looking toward the left bank Jerry saw a pair of black eyes, deep-set in a dark-skinned face, watching them from the underbrush. Startled, he felt the hair rise up on the back of his neck. Involuntarily he cried out and, pointing, drew his uncle's attention toward the figure on the shore bank. In the instant that Ed looked away, the boat veered off toward the turbulent, evil water that swirled in a nest of rocks lying between them and the shore.

A tremor passed through the hull as they slid over a submerged boulder. Then the motors ran wild as the propellers struck and sheared the pins! Ed silenced the screaming, useless engines, and without power the boat began to drift backward down the river, gaining speed as it was caught by the full force of the Kasilof's current.

## CHAPTER VI

The silence that followed the stilling of the motors was even more terrifying than the roar of the river. Jerry sat as though nailed to the seat, clutching at the gunwales of the drifting boat. Is this it, he thought? There was nothing he could do but wait it out.

Ed Carlson, though, wasn't waiting for anything. As soon as he'd shut off the motors he grabbed the oars from the top of the load and thrust them into the locks. He was standing up now, looking over his shoulder, guiding the boat stern-first down through the rapids and edging it in toward the bank. Then they were out of the fast water and as they entered an eddy that lay below the nest of rocks he put all his weight against one oar, back-watered with the other, and swung the heavy boat around until the bow pointed downstream. With a dozen or so hearty strokes he helped the current drive her hard aground onto a gravel bar.

"Boy, I sure thought we were goners there for a while!" Jerry exclaimed when they were ashore. "What happened, anyway?"

"I didn't keep my eyes on the road," Ed said, then added, "Don't ever again do anything to divert the pilot's attention when you're in white water. We were lucky that time, it could have been a lot worse."

"I guess I goofed again," Jerry said unhappily.

"No, you didn't goof, Jerry. I'm the one who goofed by not warning you. Just what were you yelling about and pointing at?"

"Well, I was just sitting there and all of a sudden I saw a kid standing in the bushes on the bank watching us. I think he was an Indian."

"An Indian kid? Where?"

Jerry pointed upstream. "Up there just beyond that big tree with the white bark."

"Beyond the birch, you mean?"

"I guess it's a birch."

Ed shaded his eyes against the sun. "Are you sure you weren't just seeing things?"

Jerry shook his head. "No, sir! He was there all right."

"I wonder what an Indian kid would be doing up here, anyway." Ed took out his pipe and tobacco. "The natives hardly ever get out of sight of the salt water."

"There was somebody there, I'd swear to that, and he sure looked like an Indian kid."

"Well," Ed said when he had his pipe lighted, "let's trot up there and see if he's still around."

Parting the salmonberry bushes and devil's club before them with their hands, they followed the old Russian boat trail up the river bank. When they had reached the gnarled birch tree that stood with limbs overhanging the current, Ed stopped and looked around. "Is this where you think you saw him?"

"Right in here someplace," Jerry said, looking about. Glancing down he saw footprints in the muddy trail. "Say, here's some tracks, and they look fresh!"

Ed came over and stood looking down at the footprints. "They are fresh, aren't they?" he said. "And just about kid-size, too." He looked around again. "Well, he can't be too far away, but if it was an Indian who made them, he could be mighty hard to find." He puffed on his pipe a few times then said, "I'd still like to know what an Indian kid would be doing up here on Silver Salmon—especially at this time of the year."

A movement in the forest background caught Jerry's eye. He took hold of his uncle's arm and when Ed looked around he nodded toward the shadowy form and said in a low voice, "There he is now, over behind that clump of bushes."

"Why, it's Joe Kashook!" Ed exclaimed. When the boy came out of hiding, he said, "You're a long way from home, aren't you, Joe?"

"I guess so."

"Why did you try to hide from me?"

"Scared, I guess," the boy answered.

"Why should you be scared of me? I've known you ever since you were born. And your dad is just about the best friend I've got."

Joe Kashook nodded.

"What are you doing up here at Silver Salmon, Joe? Aren't you supposed to be with your folks at their fishing locations down on Humpy Point?"

The boy shook his head. "We ain't fishin'."

"Not fishing? How is your dad going to make a living if he doesn't fish?"

Joe Kashook looked down and remained silent.

"You don't have to act so mysterious with me, Joe; what's he going to do?"

The boy shook his head. "I ain't supposed to tell."

Jerry had always had the opinion that Indians were dull, stupid creatures. He was surprised by the intelligent look in the native boy's eyes.

"Where is your dad, anyway?" Ed asked the boy.

"Up at Hong Kong Bend."

"What's he doing there?"

"Campin'."

"And what are you doing down here on Silver Salmon?"

"Huntin' porcupines."

"Your folks must be out of grub if they're eating porcupines. Why are they camping at Hong Kong Bend; there's nothing there."

"We run out of gas up there a couple of days ago."

"And where were you going when you ran out of gas?"

"Up the river."

"Where up the river?"

"Tustumena Lake."

"And what were you going to Tustumena Lake for?"

Joe Kashook brushed his long, uncut hair out of his eyes, shrugged and said nothing.

"You must know why your dad is going to the lake."

"He's goin' to work for Gus Kramer, I guess."

"Gus Kramer? What's he going to do for Gus, anyway?"

Joe shrugged his narrow shoulders again. "Gus said he was goin' to give us lots of money, that's all I know." The boy grinned.

Ed swore, half under his breath. "Your dad ought to know you can't believe a word Gus Kramer says. Why, I wouldn't trust him any further than I could throw a moose by the tail."

"Who is Gus Kramer?" Jerry asked.

"He's a cat-skinner by trade."

"A what?"

"A cat-skinner—tractor driver. He does a little fishing and trapping when construction work is slow, but from what I've seen of him he's an all-around shady operator. He's only been around here a couple of years but just about everybody in the district has had trouble with him already. He jumped Anvil Bergen's place on the lower river when he first came. Anvil had lived there for forty years but hadn't bothered to file for homestead rights on the property. Anvil had the last word, though; Gus gave him thirty days to get his house off the place, so Anvil burned it down and moved in with me. All Gus was after was the cabin—and without it the land wasn't worth much, anyway."

Jerry exploded. "Don't they have any laws up here to protect people from guys like that?"

"The sad part about it is that everything Gus has done so far has been a hundred per cent legal."

"How can you take a man's land and say it's legal?"

"Well, Jerry, when I first came to Alaska we used to

mind our own business and let the other fellow mind his. If a man built a house on a piece of ground he liked, everybody figured it was his and that was that; there was enough land for everybody. It was the same way with trap lines, mining claims and fishing locations. In the past few years, though, a lot of newcomers have come into the state. There's been laws passed that we never heard about; and some bird like Gus Kramer, who's got no conscience, can come along and take about everything you've got. And the government will back him up if he does it legal."

"Well, it doesn't sound fair to me!"

"What is legal isn't always fair, but you can't go around taking the law into your own hands. Some day, though, Gus is going to lock horns with the wrong guy, and then it'll be too bad for him."

"Have you ever had any trouble with him?"

"Not so far, I haven't." Ed knocked the ashes from his pipe and put it away. "Well, come on, boys, let's get back to the boat and be on our way. I want to get up to Hong Kong Bend and have a talk with Mike Kashook and find out what's been going on around here. If Gus Kramer has anything to do with it, it won't be good."

Jerry and Joe Kashook followed Ed back down the trail to where the boat was beached. Ed took out a canvas bag of tools and replaced the broken shear pin. Then he refilled the gasoline tanks. "Those motors sure must take a lot of gas," Jerry remarked. "You just filled them a little while ago."

"Oh, they didn't take much this time but I never

leave the bank without full tanks—you never can tell when you'll need that little bit extra. Ready to go?"

"As ready as I'll ever be," Jerry said.

Ed primed the motors for a quick start. "All right, Joe, you climb in back here with me. Jerry, you give the boat a good hard shove out into the current and jump aboard. You'll have to make it fast because once I'm off the bank I won't be able to come back for you if you miss. O.K., shove!"

Jerry put his weight against the bow and pushed until he was knee-deep in the river. Then as the current caught the stern and began to pivot the craft, he threw himself into the boat. The instant the bow was pointed upstream Ed jerked both starting handles at once. The motors roared to life, and once again they were on their way—working through the ugly rapids.

This time, though, Jerry didn't feel the cold, gripping terror he'd known before they had hit the rock. He was still aware of the river's dangers, but he'd gained new confidence in his uncle's ability to handle the unexpected situations that might come up. And he realized this was an ability that came from long years of practice and experience. Ed Carlson was just an ordinary human like himself, capable of error. Yet he was man enough to admit that he'd goofed when he'd run the boat into the rocks; and by the admission he'd gained stature in his nephew's eyes.

They made headway slowly for a time, then the channel became less steep and the water not so swift. As the boat stopped its pitching and bucking and the spray ceased to break inboard, Jerry began to take notice of the surrounding terrain. Once he saw a glistening, wet black bear scurrying into the underbrush carrying a flopping salmon in its jaws. Some distance beyond, a great, droopy-nosed cow moose stood knee-deep in a quiet back slough, munching on a water-lily root, while nearby her skinny, trembly-legged calf watched them timidly.

Then they rounded a long, sweeping turn where the river ran swift and deep, up close to the left hand bank. Ed shouted, "Hong Kong Bend!" and steered out of the current into the mouth of a small creek. He ran aground beside an old boat that had once been green but, weather-worn and scarred, was badly in need of repairs and a new paint job. They got out of their boat and walked toward the patched tent that stood on the grassy bank a little way back from the river. Ed called a greeting and a short, broad-shouldered man, dark-skinned and with almost oriental features, came out to meet them. A woman of the same blood and wearing a man's work-clothing was tending a red-fleshed salmon that cooked over the coals of a small fire in front of the tent.

"Hello, Mike," Ed said as he and the Indian shook hands. "Long time no see." He introduced Jerry. "I'd like to have you meet my sister's boy, Jerry Nelson. He's come up from the Outside to help out on the claim this summer. Jerry, this is Mike Kashook, Joe's father, and this is Anna, his wife." The Indian woman looked up and nodded then went on tending the broiling fish.

When the introductions had been completed, Mike

Kashook said, "How come you got my boy with you, Ed?"

"We saw him standing on the bank when we were coming through Silver Salmon. We sheared our pins about then, so as long as we had to go ashore anyway, we picked him up and brought him along."

"You fellas hungry?" the Indian asked. "We're goin' to eat pretty quick."

Jerry's uncle glanced at the fish sputtering over the fire. "Thanks a lot, Mike," he said, "but we ate just before we left the lower river, and I'm not hungry myself. How about you, Jerry?"

Jerry looked at the fish and breathed deeply of its pleasing aroma. It was not a large salmon and it might have fed two people had they not been very hungry. But this morning his appetite was such that he could have eaten the whole fish himself. But by the looks of things around the crude camp he assumed this was all the food the Indians had—the one salmon. "No, thanks," he said, "I'm not a bit hungry, either."

Jerry saw his uncle glance toward him with a faint smile and an almost imperceptible nod of his head. For a fellow who wasn't overly generous with signs of approval Ed picked the darndest times to look pleased.

Ed took out his tobacco and filled his pipe. "Joe tells me you ran out of gas, Mike." He offered his tobacco to the Indian.

Mike Kashook took the pouch and filled and lighted his own pipe before answering. "You know, Ed," he said, "this is the first time I ever run out of gas on the river. Always I make it all the way to the lake with plenty left over. I can't figure it out."

Ed puffed at his pipe for a moment and stood looking out at the Kasilof rushing past. "Well, the river is still pretty high now, Mike. The current will eat your gas up in a hurry."

"Maybe that's where I figured wrong. I never been up here in the spring before—always it's in the fall when the water is low."

"You know, I'm kind of surprised seeing you up here. I understand you're not going to fish this season."

Mike grinned. "No more fishin' for me, Ed. I give my fishin' gear and my locations to my brother. Next year he can have my boat and motors and tent and everything. I'm all through with that business for good."

"You talk like you're in the chips."

"Yes, sir," Mike said, proudly, "I'm goin' to make me big money—lots of big money. Goin' to buy me a big car this fall, new rifle, new boat with a cabin on it and new motors. Goin' to build a new house. Everybody have new clothes, too. Old lady get fur coat."

"Where are you going to get all this big money, anyway? I'd like to get my hooks into some of it, too."

Mike didn't speak for a long moment then said, "I'm goin' in partners with Gus Kramer."

"Well, that's nice. Doing what?"

"He's got him a gold claim up at Tustumena Glacier. He says he'll give me half interest if I help work it."

"For Pete's sake, Mike, you know Gus hasn't any claim up at Tustumena Glacier. Anvil Bergen and I are the only people who have any claims up there. Are you sure you understood him right? Maybe he meant some other place."

"I heard him all right. He stopped here yesterday mornin' goin' up and said he'd see me at the glacier when I got there."

"Why didn't he give you some gas if he was here?"

"All he had was diesel oil."

Ed was silent for a moment and Jerry said, "What would he do with diesel oil up there?"

"That's what I'd like to know."

Ed addressed the Indian again, "What's he going to do with the diesel oil?"

Mike shrugged. "I don't know but he sure had a load of it in his boat—ten, twelve barrels, maybe."

"Ten or twelve barrels of diesel oil but no gasoline. Something is sure screwy."

"He just had enough gas for his own motors, that's all."

"If you're going to be his partner you'd think he would at least have been able to spare you enough to get you to Slackwater. You could have sailed the rest of the way from there."

"He said somebody would come along and I could borrow some."

"That sounds like Gus Kramer, all right."

"Maybe I can borrow a little from you, huh, Ed?"

"I guess I can let you have some. Will ten gallons get you there?"

"Ten gallons is plenty."

They went to the boat and Jerry got out two five-gallon cans of gasoline and set them on the bank. "You'd better hand up a few cans of beans and a couple of tins of condensed milk, too, Jerry," Ed said. He gave the food to the Indian.

"I'll pay you back for sure when I get my big money after the cleanup," Mike said.

"You pay me back when you can," Ed said.

Jerry and his uncle waited while the Indian family ate their fish and beans, and drank the milk. When they were finished they took down their tent and stowed their meager equipment aboard the green boat. After Mike Kashook had filled his tanks and was on his way up the river, Ed knocked the ashes from his pipe. "You know, Jerry," he said thoughtfully, "there's sure something funny going on up there. Somebody is going to get taken for a sleigh ride and you can bet your sweet life it won't be Gus Kramer. Mike doesn't know it, but there's sure going to be trouble if anybody's claim gets jumped—by Gus or anybody else."

"Do you think he's jumped somebody's claim?"

"That remains to be seen. I don't think he'd dare pull anything on Anvil again, not after that other deal."

"What about your claim?"

"All my claims are staked out as legal as it's possible to do it." Ed climbed into the boat. "Come on," he said, "let's get on our way. I want to find out what that bird is up to."

## CHAPTER VII

"Did you ever run an outboard motor?" Ed asked when they were ready to leave Hong Kong Bend.

"Never anything as big as those," Jerry said, indicating the two heavy-duty engines on the stern of the boat.

"This is as good a time as any to learn. How about you taking her the rest of the way up the river?"

From the moment he'd seen the boat Jerry had been wanting to try his hand at running it and had planned to ask for the chance when they reached quiet water. But in the rapids—well, that was something else again. "Maybe I'd better wait until we get to the lake," he suggested.

"Here on the river is where you need the experience," Ed said. "Anybody can run a boat on the lake."

"Do you think I can do it?"

"Sure you can do it. From here on there's nothing to it. As a rule you take the outside of the bends and go up the middle of the straight stretches. Stay away from the riffles because they mean shallow water. And watch out for humps in the current—humps have rocks under them. I'll sit up in the bow and point out where to go."

A glance at the white water rushing past shook Jerry's confidence. "But what if something goes wrong, what if the motors quit or I hit a rock or something?" he asked.

"You saw what I did down in Silver Salmon. Shut the throttles off and grab the oars. Keep the bow pointed upstream and let the current take her into the bank. As long as you can keep her from going broadside you don't have too much to worry about."

"But what if it *does* go broadside?"

"Then you'd better get ready to take a swim." Ed showed him how to start the motors and Jerry tried it once with the boat still tied to the bank. Then his uncle said, "Here we go!" and before Jerry could change his mind Ed had shoved the craft out into the river. "Now!" he shouted, and Jerry jerked the handles, the motors came to life and they began breasting the current.

For the first few yards he was terrified, but as he felt the power at his command his confidence began to return. He moved the steering tiller slightly to the right to get the feel of the boat and was thrilled to see the bow move to the left. He moved the tiller the other way and the bow came back again. Ed looked back, nodded encouragingly and grinned. "Open 'em up!" he hollered.

Jerry shoved the throttles to the wide-open position and the boat surged ahead. As the river began to bend to the right, his uncle pointed toward the left. Jerry steered into the deep water close to the bank and skimmed so close to shore that now and then a bush scraped the boat's side. While not entirely free of his fears, he was experiencing a great sense of excitement. This, he felt, was a man's job and he didn't seem to be doing it badly at all.

As they came out of the bend and the river ahead straightened, his uncle pointed over the bow and Jerry steered the big dory up the middle of the channel, skirting boulders, riffles and occasionally a toppled tree. He swung confidently in close beside a shallow but was frightened half out of his wits as the lower end of one of the motors scraped along the bottom for an instant. "Don't get smart!" Ed yelled and waved him away from the shallow; but already Jerry had cut back out into the deeper water. After that he took it more cautiously. There was more to this, he realized, than whipping a car in and out of traffic. Down home if you got to squirreling and cutting corners, you might dent a fender or perhaps get a ticket. Here on the Kasilof, the stakes were vastly greater and the consequences much more serious. He wouldn't try *that* again.

An hour and a half after leaving Hong Kong Bend they saw the last of the rapids and Ed called out, "Slackwater!" Then they entered a long, narrow passage of smooth water, neither river nor lake but a combination of both. Several miles down the natural canal they passed a low-roofed, weathered cabin that stood on the left hand bank and a few minutes later Jerry caught his breath as the forest walls fell away on either side and they came out abruptly onto Tustumena Lake. Beyond the right hand shore of the broad expanse of milky-green water were wooded foothills. To the left, jagged, formidable mountains formed a barrier along the eastern skyline. But the thing that thrilled Jerry, caught and held his eye, was the great tongue of blue ice that spilled out of a canyon at the far end of the lake. The glacier seemed to grow in size as they neared it until it appeared to fill half the sky ahead.

When they stopped to refuel, Ed said, "Maybe I'd better take over for the rest of the way. It looks like we just might run into a blow before too long." Jerry was glad to be in the bow again. When they were about halfway down the lake he began to see whitecaps ahead, then a gust of sharp, biting wind hit him in the face. The boat started tossing and pitching as the water roughened, and spray began breaking inboard. Long before the first puff of wind was upon them, Ed had changed course and headed for the protection of a small bay. When they reached the calm water behind a point of land that thrust out from the right hand shore, he shut the motors off and Jerry threw the anchor overboard.

The treetops on the shore were nodding and bowing to one another, and when the engine roar had faded from their ears, they could hear the sound of the wind. "That wind is what we call a williwaw," Ed said. "The whole Pacific Ocean lies just beyond those mountains over there and some say it's the warm winds blowing off the water onto the ice that causes them. I don't know, but they're especially bad at this time of the year. The wind just starts whooping and howling all of a sudden and it can pile up some pretty nasty waves so the only thing to do is hole up until she blows over. It generally only lasts an hour or two, and when it has died down the lake will be as calm as a platter again. But don't ever try to buck a williwaw, Jerry. Just get in behind the nearest shelter and stay there till it's over—even if you have to sit for a week."

They opened some cans of food and had a cold meal while they waited for the wind to abate. "What did you think of Tustumena Glacier?" Ed asked when they were finished.

"It sure has a beautiful blue color, but it looks as though it would be awfully cold."

"It isn't bad at all up there. In fact the sun reflecting off the ice can get downright uncomfortable at times."

"And just where is the claim?"

"Right up against the foot of the ice, as close to it as I can get."

"Why so close?"

"First of all, let me tell you something about a glacier, Jerry. That's not just a big hunk of dead ice lying there. A glacier is alive; it's always moving, grinding the mountains down and carrying them bit by bit down toward sea level. It might take millions of years to do it, but a glacier will destroy anything that gets in its way. When there are cold cycles in the climate, the ice advances; and when a warm cycle comes along, it melts away and draws itself back into the mountains. When Anvil Bergen first saw Tustumena Lake, the end of the ice was almost down to the water. Now look at it. You have to hike close to three miles across the flats to get to her. What does that mean to you?"

Jerry thought for a moment. "Well, that must mean the weather has been getting warmer."

"Right. Now each time the glacier melts back, it drops the load of rocks and dirt and dust it carries. When it advances, it brings down another load of the stuff it grinds out of that canyon back there. I've dug test holes all over the moraine that lies between the glacier and the lake, and all the way to bedrock you can see the stratas of sediment the glacier deposited each time that it receded. And in each strata you find 'color,' that is, little particles of gold. The color down at the edge of the lake is as fine as flour. That's because it was carried the furthest and has had more time to be ground up between the ice and the rocks. The closer you get to the glacier itself the coarser the gold becomes. Do you know what *that* means?"

"Is it because the gold hasn't been carried so far and hasn't had a chance to be ground up?"

"Right again—you're learning fast. Now here's my theory: Last year hardly any of the nuggets I took out showed signs of having been carried very far. About all of the gold had sharp corners and looked as though it had just been dug out of a vein. There was a lot of sharp-edged quartz in with it, too. If the glacier melts back as far this summer as it did last year, then I'd say that before freeze-up we'll find the lode where she's been picking up the gold."

"The big strike, you mean?"

"Right. I found a little brass flask of nuggets one time in the old Russian ruins, and it was all sharp, new gold like I was getting last year. It's my opinion that in the Russian days the foot of the glacier was further back than it is now. It just might even be possible they worked the lode we're looking for before the climate got colder and the glacier advanced again and covered up their diggings."

"Couldn't you dig back under the glacier instead of waiting for it to melt?"

Ed shook his head. "Too dangerous. The ice would cave in your hole or else it would fill up with water faster than you could ever pump it out. No, sir, Jerry, the safest way is the slow way. We'll just let Mother Nature do the work and if we don't hit it this year, there'll always be next year, or the next."

"I thought about everybody had switched over to hunting for uranium these days," Jerry commented.

"Yes, a lot of the prospectors have thrown away their gold pans and are running around the hills with Geiger counters. In fact, I took a fling at it myself for a little while a couple of years ago but once you've seen gold in a sluice box you can never be content with anything else."

"Isn't there a lot more money to be made in uranium?"

"Maybe—that is, if you find it. But you know, Jerry, there's more to this prospecting business than the money you get out of it. I'd have quit looking for gold a long time ago if money had been my only interest. No, sir, it's the looking for it that keeps a man going. Why I'd rather shovel gravel all day for a dollar's worth of dust than to make fifty doing anything else."

"I don't get it," Jerry said, unable to grasp his uncle's reasoning.

"You will when you find your first nugget." Ed looked out toward the lake. "Well, it looks like she's about all over, Jerry. Get that anchor up and we'll be on our way." Jerry took hold of the wet rope and pulled the anchor up. Then Ed started the motors and they continued their journey down the lake toward the glacier.

Two hours later the dory left the milky lake water and entered the mouth of a crystal clear creek. Not far away, Jerry could see a big log house that stood in a clearing at the edge of the forest. There was a large, barn-like structure near the house and through an open, second-story window Jerry could see hay sticking out. Beyond the barn was a small cabin built up on poles well above the ground. Jerry recognized it from pictures he'd seen as a "cache" where extra food and supplies were stored to keep them above the reach of marauding animals. Two black horses were grazing on the bank of the creek. They stopped feeding and stood with ears erect, watching the approaching boat.

A lean, wiry little man with a rugged, weather-tanned face and thick, white hair came out of the house at their approach. Ed shut the motors off and ran the boat hard ashore alongside a gray dory and called out, "Hello, Anvil! How's everything?"

"I'm all right, Ed," the old man answered, "but I'm sure glad you got back when you did!"

"How come—have you got troubles of some kind?"

"Gus Kramer has jumped your No. 4 claim!"

Jerry's heart leaped at the words. So Gus *had* jumped his uncle's claim. He wondered what that was going to mean. What was going to be done about it?

"He can't jump any of my claims," Ed said angrily as he got out of the boat. "I've always done everything just the way the law says it's supposed to be done."

"I know, I know," Anvil replied, shaking his head, "but that fellow has never yet been wrong when it comes to the law."

"This time he *is* wrong. Just how did it all happen, anyway, Anvil? What did he do?"

"Well, a day or so after you left here I decided I'd go up to the diggin's and patch up the wanigan and maybe start sluicing a little. When I got part way up I thought I heard a motor running and then I saw a tent set up just beyond the monument at the end of your No. 3 claim. When I got there I saw Gus up on a tractor bulldozing a channel down along the foot of the glacier so as to carry the melt water off into Glacier Creek."

"You say he's got a tractor?"

"Yes, one of the big ones."

"Then that explains the diesel oil Mike Kashook said Gus had in his boat. I wonder how he got a tractor up here?"

"The only thing I can figure is that he must have driven it in over the muskeg and across the lake during the winter when everything was all froze up—and kept her hid out in the woods till he knew you were gone."

"What happened then?"

"Well, he saw me watching him and got down off the machine and came up and said to get off his claim and to stay off. And I said, 'What do you mean, your claim? This is Ed Carlson's No. 4 you're on,' and then he said, 'You mean it *was* Ed Carlson's No. 4—it's my No. 1 now.' Then he told me if I didn't get off the claim somebody would have to carry me off. He had a pistol sticking out of his pocket, so I got."

Jerry had thought that the days of the pistol-toting desperado were long gone. But apparently in the North they were not. Perhaps this country was even more primitive than his uncle had led him to believe. The thought excited him.

"I don't like to think of any man as being a killer," Ed said, "and as much as I don't like Gus, I never thought that about him. But this pistol business—well, it's enough to make you wonder." Then he said, "Anvil, I want you to meet my nephew, Jerry Nelson. He's going to be with us this summer." To Jerry he said, "This is Anvil Bergen, the fellow I've been telling you about. His claims adjoin mine and we always help one another out. If he ever needs help you're to give it to him."

Anvil shook hands with Jerry. "I'll be able to use a big lad like you when it comes time to start muckin' —that is, if Gus doesn't figure out a way to jump my claims, too."

"We're going to put a stop to that guy," Ed said, a hardness coming into his eyes. "The more you give in to a bird like him the harder he is to handle. You've got to stop him in his tracks or he'll run all over everybody."

"Well, you figure out a way to do it and I'll go along with you," Anvil said. "I've got a special interest in him myself."

"I know you have, Anvil, but we've got to do it without any rough stuff if we can help it. Gus would just love to see us get in wrong with the law, so if there's to be any trouble we'll let him start it."

"What can you do, anyway?" Jerry asked.

His uncle looked out into the northwest where the sinking sun was reddening the sky as it went down behind the mountains beyond Cook Inlet. "We've been on the go all day long so I think we'd better get a few hours' sleep before we do anything about Gus. Maybe in the morning when we're all rested up we'll see things a little more clearly. Right now I'm too mad to think straight."

It seemed as though he'd barely closed his eyes when Jerry felt someone shaking him and heard his uncle's voice saying, "Rise and shine, young fellow! Hit the deck and wash your neck—we've got a big day ahead of us!"

Jerry felt that he could have slept for hours longer, but after washing his face and hands in cold water he was fully awake. Anvil was busy at the cookstove, and as Jerry came back inside the old man set a plate of moose steak and sourdough pancakes on the table. "Eat hearty, lad," he said. "It's better than three miles up to the diggin's and you never know what we'll run into or how long we'll be there."

After they had eaten breakfast Ed took one of the heavy rifles down from a rack made of antlers and handed it to Jerry with a box of cartridges. "Out here in the back country we never go anyplace without a rifle. So first thing this morning we're going to see if you can shoot."

"Oh, I can shoot all right," Jerry said as he loaded the rifle, "but this gun is a lot bigger than dad's 30-30." He read the calibre on the side of the barrel, ".405."

"The .405 is a bear stopper," Ed said, taking a similar rifle down from the rack and loading it. "This time of year the brownies are still hungry after their winter's hibernation and they can be mighty ugly if you should come face to face with one of them."

"Brownies?"

"Brown bear—same thing as a Kodiak."

"You mean like those great big ones that wave at you and beg for peanuts in the zoo at Woodland Park back home?"

"The same thing. Only these don't beg for peanuts—they're meat eaters."

"Well, gee, they're awfully big."

"They're the biggest bears in the world. About the meanest, too, when they get stirred up."

"And you say there are wild ones around here?"

"The woods are full of them."

Jerry looked at his uncle, then at Anvil Bergen. "Oh, you guys are kidding me, I'll bet." He laughed.

Ed shook his head and his face was deadly serious. "Brown bears aren't anything to kid about, Jerry. The woods *are* full of them, but we've learned to live with them. We leave them alone and they leave us alone. We know they like to hole up in alders so we stay out of the alders. Unless I'm on a hunt I make lots of noise when I'm out in the woods. If they hear you coming, they'll fade away and you'll never know there's one around. It's when you come on him all of a sudden that a brownie is dangerous."

"But what if you *do* come on one all of a sudden?"

"Then you'd better be a darned good shot."

Jerry hefted the .405. "Maybe I'd better have a little target practice."

"That's just what we're going to do. You were bragging that you could shoot. Now let's go out and see if you're a shooting shooter or a talking shooter."

They went outside and Anvil set some tin cans on stumps between the house and the lake, so the spent bullets would fly harmlessly off over the water. "All right, let's see how good you are," Ed said. Anvil came back and stood behind them on the porch, well out of the line of fire.

Jerry worked the lever of the rifle to put a shell into the firing chamber then threw the gun to his shoulder and, aware of the two men's eyes upon him, he snapped a quick shot at the nearest can. "BAM!" went the rifle and the recoil jarred him back on his heels. When he regained his balance he saw that the can was still in place. And from the angle at which the whistling bullet was ricocheting out over the lake, he could see that he'd missed by a mile. "My gosh, this thing kicks," he complained, lowering the rifle and rubbing his bruised shoulder. "No wonder I missed."

Ed shook his head. "It wasn't the kick that did it

because the bullet is out of the barrel before the gun recoils."

"It's a strange gun," Jerry alibied.

"Now don't go blaming the gun. For one thing you didn't even aim, but mostly you were trying to show us how good you are. The only thing that will impress anybody up here is straight shooting, not spectacular shooting."

Jerry flushed as the truth of his uncle's words sank in. He tried to think of an excuse to justify his actions but thought better of it. After all, he *had* been showing off.

"Now try it again," Ed said, "and remember that you're not performing with a .22 in a shooting gallery for the benefit of your buddies. Up here we shoot for keeps. Do it the way your dad taught you. I know *he* can shoot."

"But it kicks so darned hard."

"Well, if you're afraid of the gun then you'd better forget about it," Ed said with scorn in his voice. "Maybe we can hire a bodyguard to look after you." He turned and started for the house.

"I'm not afraid," Jerry called after him quickly.

Ed stopped and looked back over his shoulder. "Then let's see you shoot."

Jerry ejected the empty shell and loaded a fresh one. The gun was trembling as he raised it to his shoulder.

"Hey, hey!" Ed said sharply. "Hold it a second before you get your head knocked off."

Jerry lowered the gun.

"Look," Ed said, putting his own rifle to his shoulder.

"Here's why that gun hurt you—you held it too loose. Snuggle up close to it—pretend it is your best girl friend. Lay your cheek up solid against the stock and hold her good and firm—like this." He fired a shot and a can went spinning off a stump.

Jerry raised the rifle again and laid into it firmly, the way his uncle had done. He remembered now that this was the same thing his dad had told him, and he remembered, too, that he was supposed to keep his feet further apart. "Now you're getting the hang of it," Ed called encouragingly. "At least you look like a shooter. Just imagine that can is a bull moose and you haven't eaten for a week—and you've only got one shell left to your name."

Jerry found the can over the open sights, took a deep breath, held it, pulled the trigger. "BAM!" Why he hardly felt the kick at all that time, and the can had fallen from the stump. He worked the lever of the rifle and aimed at another can. "BAM!" That one went spinning, too. He hurried a little and missed with the next shot but he hit again with the last one.

"Well, not bad at all," Anvil said with a nod of approval from where he stood on the porch.

The old man's words pleased Jerry and he felt vindicated for the mess he'd made of his first shot. "Well, I haven't shot for a long time," he said.

"You've got to get better than that," his uncle said. "Three out of five isn't considered especially good shooting around here."

"Then what is?" Jerry asked, a little angry.

"You've got to be able to make it five out of five up

here to break even—or else stay clear out of the woods," Ed said. "Cliff Steele got careless and missed with his last shot—and you remember what that moose did to him."

Jerry recalled the badly crippled Alaskan who had stayed with them in Seattle for a time several years ago. Yes, maybe his uncle knew what he was talking about at that.

"Enough of this for today," Ed said when they had reloaded the rifles. "I guess we'd better be on our way if we're going to have our little chat with Mr. Kramer. Let's hit the trail."

"You have to take a boat to get to the other side of Glacier Creek now," Anvil said.

"A boat to cross Glacier Creek? Why, I've always been able to jump over it."

"Not this year you can't, Ed. Do you remember how there used to be a dozen creeks that carried the melt water away from the ice and down across the glacier flats to the lake?"

"Yes."

"Well, since Gus has bulldozed that big ditch along the face of the ice, all the water is coming down along the canyon wall and those little streams have all dried up. Glacier Creek is almost as wide and as swift as the Kasilof now."

"That's something I've wanted to do for years but I never had the machine to do it with," Ed said. "Maybe Gus is good for something after all."

"I've been watching him from up on top of the canyon wall where you've got your monuments, and I can say one thing for him, he sure knows how to handle a tractor."

"That's the unfortunate thing about Gus. Everything he does he can do better than anybody else. If he hadn't been born with that greedy streak in him, he'd be quite a man."

Carrying their guns they got into Ed's boat and ran down the shore of the lake a short distance until they were beyond the mouth of the muddy stream that was pouring great quantities of roiled water out into Tustumena Lake. "I see Mike made it all right," Ed said when they were ashore. He indicated the battered old green dory that was drawn up out of the water next to a bright yellow, shovelnose river boat.

A dozen or so steel oil barrels lay scattered about near the yellow boat, and Anvil pointed to some tracks in the sand. "Here's where he's dragged a sled down with the tractor to get his drums," he said. He went around kicking the barrels and most of them rang hollowly. "Sounds like it's about all gone except for that load he brought up a day or two ago." He thumped the full barrels that were still in the yellow shovelnose.

They took their rifles and headed toward the glacier, following the gouged-out trail made by the tractor and sled. For a short distance back from the lake shore the moraine was covered with a stand of tall birch and willow saplings. But as they neared the glacier the trees became shorter, changing to sparse underbrush, and beyond the bushes they passed through high weeds, then clumps of grass, and finally there was no vegetation at all. Off to the left they could hear the hollow roar of

Glacier Creek and see the muddy water racing along the foot of the sheer wall of the canyon that towered above their heads. Jerry noticed some long scratches ground into the face of the rock and asked about them. "Those were put there by the glacier," his uncle said. "Big rocks get frozen into the ice and as the whole thing moves, the rocks gouge those scratches into the cliff. This was under ice when Anvil came here."

"Clear down almost to the lake," Anvil added. "All those bushes and saplings back there have sprung up since I first came here."

Despite the brightness of the morning sun, Jerry could feel the cold breath of the glacier as they came near it. Ahead the blue ice reached from the canyon wall to a similar cliff a good mile off to the right. In between, all was desolate, barren gravel flats—the moraine, devoid of everything that grew or moved, reminded Jerry of a desert, dead and lifeless. As they approached the glacier he saw ahead an oblong house built on sled runners. "What's that thing?" he asked.

"That's the wanigan," his uncle said. "It's just a shack on skids that we live in while we're working on our claims. As the ice recedes we just hitch the horses to it and drag it on."

Before long they began to hear the deep-throated roar of a laboring tractor and then they saw two tents that were pitched on a bit of high ground beyond the wanigan. Jerry recognized the patched and faded one that he had seen previously at the Indian camp on the river bank down at Hong Kong Bend.

When they were within half a mile of the ice field

they came to a heap of stones that had been piled up to a height of about six feet above the surrounding terrain. Ed leaned his rifle against the stones and said, "There's no use giving Gus an excuse to start any gunplay so we'd better leave our artillery here." Anvil and Jerry put their rifles down beside Ed's.

"What's this pile of rocks for?" Jerry asked.

"This is the monument that marks the northwest corner of my No. 1 claim," Ed said. He pointed toward the rim of the canyon wall off to the left. "See those cairns up there on top of the cliff?"

Looking up Jerry could see several evenly-spaced heaps of stones standing against the skyline. "Yes."

"The first monument up there marks the northeast corner of this No. 1 claim; the second one, No. 2, and so on up the line."

Jerry counted the cairns. "Seven. I thought you only had one claim."

"The law allows me to stake out as many as I want as long as I do a hundred dollars' worth of assessment work on them each year. I've got six claims altogether, and I could stake the rest of the glacier if I wanted to, but even at the rate she's melting back now it will never reach the last monument; not in my lifetime, at least."

"How big are the claims?"

"A placer claim contains 20 acres and is 660 feet wide by 1,320 feet in length. The long way runs between here and the top of the cliff; the short way, between here and the next monument up there toward the ice. The eastern border of all my claims runs along the top of the cliff and the western border cuts from here straight ahead over the flat and across the ice until it reaches a point at right angles with the seventh monument."

"And where are your claims, Anvil?" Jerry asked.

Anvil pointed to the west toward the right hand canyon wall. "My claims all adjoin Ed's. My No. 1 starts right here and runs a quarter of a mile to that monument over there to the west and they go south as far as your uncle's last monument."

Leaving their rifles leaning against the piled-up stones they went on toward the glacier, heading in the general direction of the two tents. They passed the wanigan and stopped near the fourth pile of stones that marked the far corner of Ed's No. 3 claim. A thousand and some rivulets and trickles of milky water were running down off the end of the glacier, and the residue of ice was melting under the heat of the bright June sun. And all this water pouring into the ditch flowed eastward, growing in size until it became a raging torrent as it neared the canyon wall. Here, with his back toward them, a thick-shouldered man was driving a crawler-type tractor, scooping great loads of gravel and rocks into the angry water that rushed along between himself and the wall of ice that was the foot of Tustumena Glacier.

While they stood watching the tractor, Mike Kashook stepped out of his tent, working the lever of a rifle as he came. Pointing the gun in their direction he said, "You guys ain't supposed to be on our claim."

## CHAPTER VIII

"Anvil, you and Jerry stay right here," Ed ordered. "I'm going to see if I can talk some sense into Mike."

"Maybe we'd better go back and get the guns," Anvil said. "That kind of sense he'll understand."

"I know just how you feel, Anvil. I don't like anybody pointing a gun at me, either, but I've known Mike for a good many years and I don't think he'll give us any real trouble—I hope."

"If we had our guns here so we could back you up, I'll bet he wouldn't give you any trouble," Jerry said.

"No, let's do it my way, Jerry. You fellows wait here and I'll go on up and talk to him." Jerry and Anvil stayed where they were and watched anxiously while Ed went toward the armed Indian. When he was within a few yards of the native, Ed said, "Put your gun away, Mike, I want to talk to you."

"Gus says nobody can come past that rock pile," Mike warned, keeping the rifle pointed toward Ed.

"You can get into serious trouble threatening people with a gun, Mike. You know better than that."

"I got orders."

"Now, listen to me, Mike—"

"He don't listen to nobody but me, Mister!"

From where he stood with Anvil Jerry could hear the deep, rasping voice but was unable to see the speaker until a massive, unshaven man, seeming to be all neck and shoulders, stepped from behind one of the tents with a pistol in his hand. So this is Gus Kramer, Jerry thought, and even had he not already known of the man's reputation he would have feared him. He looked like a first class thug.

"You're the guy I really want to talk to, Gus," Ed said. "What do you think you're doing up here, anyway?"

"Workin' my claim, that's what I'm doin'."

"You know darn well that's my No. 4 you're on, Gus, and I've got two more staked out beyond that."

"Oh? Well, it's *my* No. 1 now."

Jerry and Anvil walked up until they were flanking Ed, and stood listening.

"Gus, you must be crazy. Everybody knows I staked all six of these claims twenty years ago and you can't just walk in and overstake me. It's not legal."

"Well, I've got news for you, Buster. How much assessment work have you done on this claim here, the one you call No. 4?"

"None yet, because it's been under ice up until this year. How *could* I do any assessment work on it?"

The talk between the two men got too technical for Jerry. One thing he could understand, though, was that they were both mad and at any moment he expected fists to fly.

Gus continued. "And the law says you can't hold a

claim if you don't do the assessment work. Twenty years you've had this claim staked out, and in all that time you never stuck a shovel into a square foot of it. According to the book you've got no legal right to it and anyone can come along and overstake you. Am I right, or ain't I?"

Ed didn't say anything for a moment then he turned and looked toward Anvil and Jerry and half-shrugged. "Well, I—"

Anvil shook his head. "I'm afraid he's got you there, Ed. If you don't do any assessment work on a claim, you can't hold it." Then Anvil turned to Gus and said, "How come you didn't jump my No. 4, too, while you were at it?"

"Oh, you'd already done some work on it this spring before I got here so that would make it illegal and you know I wouldn't do anything like that."

Anvil stepped up to the big man and said in a steely voice, "Gus, I don't know where you came from or what you did before you got here, but you don't belong in this district."

"What you or anybody else thinks of me is the least of my worries. And, furthermore, I guess I've as much right here as anybody."

"You're a downright thief!"

"Well, now, you listen to me, Bergen. Any time you catch me breakin' the law you just call in the United States marshal and let him take care of it. And until then I'd just as soon you stayed off my property and kept your nose out of my business. The law gives me the right to protect my claim against trespassers and as of now you're all trespassin'. And like I told you before, if you don't get off quick and stay off, then somebody will get carried off."

While he had no way of knowing whether the big man was right or wrong, Jerry had the impression that Gus was trying to run a bluff. In any case he intended to help resist *anyone's* efforts to take his uncle's claim away including Gus Kramer. Suddenly he saw fire come into Anvil's eyes and the old man's clenched fist started to swing.

But Gus had seen it, too, and he let fly a blow that sent Anvil sprawling into the gravel. Ed headed for Gus but the heavy-set man pointed the pistol at his stomach. "Stay where you're at, Carlson."

Ed stopped.

"Now let's get something straight right now," Gus said, menacing them all with the gun. "I've filed on this claim and they tell me up at Anchorage that she's mine as long as I work her every year. So get off and keep off. And don't any of you go comin' around here sometime when I'm gone because my partner will be lookin' out for his interests, too, won't you, Mike?"

Mike Kashook glanced toward them out of the corner of his eye then back at Gus and said, "Sure, sure, you and me are partners. We'll keep 'em off."

Ed stepped back over the imaginary line that lay between the nearby monument and the one on the clifftop. "You know, Mike," he said, "I could expect something like this from Kramer here. But you and I have been friends for a long time—you've helped me and

I've helped you—and I never thought I'd see the day you'd turn on me."

"He's got to protect his interests, the same as me," Gus said, fingering his weapon.

Mike wouldn't look Ed in the eye but stood staring down at the ground and said, "Yeah, we got to protect our interests."

Anvil got to his feet and brushed the dust off his clothes. He was grumbling under his breath when Ed turned his back on Gus and Mike Kashook. "Come on, boys," he said, "let's get out of here. Somehow I don't like the smell of the place anymore."

Jerry was so angry he was ready to fight, guns or no guns, and as they walked away from the disputed claim he said, bitterly, "That's gratitude for you."

"What do you mean?" his uncle asked.

"Well, when that Indian was stranded and hungry you gave him gas and food—and now he pays you back by siding in against you with a crook like Gus Kramer."

"I know how you feel," Ed said. He put a calming hand on Jerry's shoulder as they walked along, side by side. "It always hurts to have someone you like let you down, but when you look right at it, Mike Kashook doesn't owe me a thing. The natives live only for today and have little understanding of the meaning of tomorrow. To Mike, Gus represents an opportunity for food and shelter, right here and now. Sure, you and I know that Gus is only going to use him for his own interests and when he has no more need for him he'll toss Mike out on his ear. All through history it's been the same; every time the Indian comes into contact with the white man something is taken from him; his home, his lands, his freedom, even his life, so why shouldn't the native take what he can get whenever he can get it? No, Jerry, don't blame poor Mike Kashook; it's the white men who are to blame."

"I guess I never thought of it that way before," Jerry said, "but that doesn't excuse Gus."

"That's right. If you have to be sore at somebody make it be Gus and you'll have a lot of company."

"You know, just looking at that guy scares me."

"That's his chief stock in trade—his ugly face and belligerent attitude. But I honestly believe that if you caught him out without a gun, man to man, you'd find him just like most bullies—all bluff and no guts."

"Well, I wouldn't want to tangle with him myself."

"And I don't blame you for that."

They went back to the first monument and got their rifles and no one said anything more for a time as they walked toward the boat they had left on the shore of the lake. But when they came to the beach Ed slapped his thigh and looked up with a grin. "I don't know why I'm wasting my time thinking about what I can do to get even with Gus Kramer—whether he knows it or not he's about the best friend we ever had."

Anvil looked hard into Ed's eyes. "You don't look crazy but you sure talk like you've missed too many boats."

"Gus might be a whiz of a cat-skinner and a mighty sharp operator, but he's no miner, that's for sure."

"He was going about it like he knew what he was doing."

"Sure, he's dug a nice big ditch so he can use all the water running off the ice to sluice the gold out of the gravel and that's the thing to do. But think hard now, Anvil, what was there about his operation that was all wrong?"

Anvil stopped and stood looking off into the distance for a time then said, "You've got me, Ed. What *was* he doing wrong?"

Jerry's uncle picked up a piece of driftwood and drew a rough diagram in the damp sand of the beach. "Here's the glacier here," he said, making a line, "and here's the cliff over here to the left." He made some rectangles. "Here's my No. 3 claim and here's the No. 4—what Gus calls his No. 1—and off here to the right is your No. 4."

"That's just the way it is, all right," Anvil said.

Ed handed the stick to Jerry. "Here, you put Gus Kramer's ditch on that little map for us, will you, Jerry?"

Jerry took the stick and thought for a moment then said, "As I remember, it starts here at the edge of Anvil's No. 4, up against the ice."

"Right. Go ahead, draw in the rest of it."

"Then it goes over here along the foot of the glacier and just before it gets to the cliff it turns left—"

Ed interrupted. "That turn is important, Jerry; isn't it a little more this way?"

"That's right, it was just about in line with the cairns."

"Ha, ha!" Anvil exploded. "I get it now! I see what you're driving at, Ed. Oh, boy, is he dumb!"

"I don't get it," Jerry said, looking puzzled.

"You've got to be a miner to get it, Jerry," Ed said. "Let me explain something to you. In placer mining you're after the loose gold that's mixed up with the dirt and gravel and about the best way to get it is to dump the pay dirt into a stream of running water. Now gold is very heavy; and as the water carries the dirt along, the gold sinks faster and settles to the bottom while the gravel and everything else is carried on."

"Isn't that what he's doing?"

"In a small operation you use a long, narrow sluice box with boards called riffles nailed crossways in the bottom. The riffles slow the water down just enough to catch the gold and hold it there. Anything that will slow water in a sluice will stop the gold. The thing that Gus is doing wrong is that he's got his ditch too big and too steep and the water is running too fast and he's got no riffles. So every speck of gold will keep sliding along the bottom until it gets to this turn here." Ed put his finger on the sketch he'd drawn in the sand. "The bend in the ditch will slow the water down and the gold will stop right about there."

"Inside the boundary of your No. 3 claim?" Jerry asked.

"Just inside!" Ed said, and Anvil roared again.

"You sure have got a nice fellow working for you back there, Ed," the old man said, slapping Jerry's uncle on the back.

"Was he right when he said he could keep trespassers off?" Jerry asked.

"That's right, if he has a legal claim," Ed said.

"And then you can keep him off your No. 3, too, can't you?"

"What's sauce for the goose is sauce for the gander."

Jerry pointed to the diagram. "Then how is he going to get out if you don't want him to? There's the cliff over there on the east and the glacier is to the south; Anvil's No. 4 has him boxed in on the west and if you don't let him across your No. 3 how is he going to get off that No. 1 of his—your No. 4, I mean?"

Ed looked at the diagram, then at Anvil and grinned broadly. "Yes, sir, it looks like Gus has really cooked his own goose this time."

When they got back to the cabin Ed took a book down from a shelf and read a page over to himself. "I knew I was right all the time," he said. "Listen to what the mining laws say about assessment work: 'Where a number of contiguous claims are held in common, the aggregate expenditure for the group may be made on one claim, provided such expenditure tends to benefit or develop each claim of the group'."

Anvil looked puzzled then said, "Some of those words are kind of big for me, Ed."

"And for me, too," Jerry said. "What does it mean in plain language?"

"Well, it means just this, as I get it: I can do the assessment work for all six claims on one claim providing the work on that one benefits all the rest."

"But I'm just wondering," Anvil said, "how the work you've done so far on your No. 1, 2 and 3 can be of any benefit to 4, 5 and 6 when they're covered with a hundred feet or so of ice."

Jerry's uncle frowned. "That's just the fine point of the law where Gus might have me licked. So I think I'd better get up to Anchorage and see a good mining lawyer before I do anything about trying to get him off."

"Well, I don't think he's got a leg to stand on, myself," Anvil said, "but you better play it safe and find out for sure."

"And what will you do if he is wrong?" Jerry asked.

"If I'm in the right, I'll just have to take Gus's advice and swear out a warrant for claim jumping and have the U. S. marshal come down and put him off. But until then we'll leave him alone. He can't do any harm to the claim and he might make some improvements with that tractor of his that will save us a lot of pick and shovel work later on."

"When are you going to leave?" Anvil asked.

"Just as soon as I can get a bite to eat. I'll be in Anchorage by evening and if I can see the lawyer first thing in the morning I should be back here by tomorrow night."

"Is there anything you'd like me to do while you're gone?" Jerry asked.

Ed looked at him for a moment with another of his rare pleased-looking expressions and said, "Well, all the supplies will have to be packed up to the wanigan, that's the most important thing."

"And when we get that done we'll set up the sluice boxes," Anvil said. "Where do you want to start muckin'?"

"The pay streak is bound to be richest nearest to the

ice. So you might as well start as close to the boundary between No. 3 and No. 4 as you can. But be sure you don't touch a pebble on the No. 4 or step over the line. We want to have our hands clean if there's going to be any legal trouble."

"And what about Gus?" Jerry asked. "What will we do if he wants to come across?"

Ed thought for a moment, then said, "I kind of hate to pen a man in there against the ice like that, but—"

"Well, he can't come across my claims, I'll tell you that," Anvil said bitterly.

"We'll have to stick together on it, then. You have my authority to keep him off, and if he does try to come across, tell him we'll talk about access rights when I get back. But don't let him on the No. 3 until then."

"Good," Anvil said. "If he wants to play dirty, so can we."

They ate their noontime meal, and Ed left immediately afterwards heading his boat for the west end of the lake and the Kasilof River. Jerry began helping to load supplies into Anvil's boat, a large, open dory similar to his uncle's.

"Before Gus turned all that water loose in Glacier Creek," the old man said, "we used to be able to load up the horses here at the cabin and wade 'em across and go right on up to the claims. Now we've got to boat everything over to the other side of the creek and pack in from there. It means handling everything twice but it's got to be done. At least that's better than backpackin' everything like we did in the old days."

"Can't we run the boat up the creek to the claims?"

Anvil shook his head. "I tried it a couple of days ago but she's just a bit too swift. No, sir, thanks to Gus Kramer it looks like we'll have to do it the hard way."

They took a boatload of supplies down to the landing beyond Glacier Creek, then came back for the pack saddles, sacks of oats and bales of hay. Jerry operated the boat and Anvil led the horses down the beach to the mouth of the stream and swam them across to the other side. They dried the animals off with sacks, then Anvil put the pack saddles onto their backs and he and Jerry loaded them with supplies. The made two round trips between the lake and the No. 3 claim, and Jerry was bone-tired and about ready to drop. "Well, lad, you've done a pretty fair day's work today," Anvil said. "Let's call it quits. We'll have to bring the rest of the stuff up tomorrow."

"I'm about dead," Jerry said. "I'm not used to hiking over rocks all day."

"Those city pavements will ruin anybody's feet," Anvil told him. "But you'll get broken in and be in first class shape in a few days." They went into the wanigan and Anvil started a fire in the small oil stove in one corner. "Maybe you better go take care of the horses while I fix us a bite to eat," he said as Jerry sat down and started to untie his shoes. "Give 'em each a nosebag of oats and a big armload of hay, then rub them down good and after they're all cooled off, take them down to the creek and let them have a drink of water."

"I think I'll rest for a while first," Jerry remarked. "I've had a pretty rough day of it." He kicked his shoes off.

"The horses have had a rough day of it, too," Anvil said.

"Yes, but they're used to it."

Anvil looked him in the eye for a moment then said, "All right, if you're that tired I'll do it for you." He hesitated a moment then added, "But your supper will be a bit late."

As he reached for his shoes Jerry wished he could fall through the floor to hide his embarrassment. It wasn't so much what the kindly-faced old man had said but the way that he'd said it. And this wasn't the first time it had happened, either. These men up here were different from the ones back home. When they said something they meant business, and they had a way of making you feel like a five-year-old if you didn't measure up. But how was he to know that up here the horses come first?

When he came out of the wanigan the Kashook family was watching him from the area in front of their tent. He hadn't seen Gus since they'd had the run-in with him earlier in the day. But he could hear the tractor working near the ridge of gravel that lay between the wanigan and the glacier. Jerry hung the nosebags on the horses' heads and while they munched at their oats, he got sacks and began rubbing them down. In the midst of his work he heard the tractor go silent and a few minutes later Gus came up over the ridge beyond the tents and stood talking with Mike Kashook. They were too far away for him to hear what was being said but he could tell by the way they kept looking in his direction that they were discussing him. Anna

Kashook came out of one of the tents with a cooking pot in her hand. She said something to the men and they followed her back inside. Probably going in for their dinner, he thought.

When the horses had cooled off, Jerry led them toward the creek to drink.

## CHAPTER IX

"Ed tells me your folks have been a little concerned about you, lad," Anvil said when Jerry came back to the wanigan. He put the biscuits in the oven and sat down with his pipe. "But I don't think they've got too much to worry about."

Jerry was embarrassed by Anvil's words but he also felt a warm glow. It was good to have the old man's approval, even if he didn't deserve it.

"But next time—" Anvil was interrupted by the roaring of Gus Kramer's tractor engine.

"Sounds as though he's coming up out of the ditch," Jerry said.

Anvil got up from his seat and looked out a window of the wanigan. "Holy smoke, lad, we've got to get out of here! Gus has got a sledload of oil barrels hitched on behind his cat and he's coming right at us!" Anvil grabbed his rifle and ran out of the door with Jerry close behind him. Outside, Anvil planted himself between the wanigan and the advancing tractor and raised the gun. "That's far enough!" he shouted.

Gus stopped the tractor. "I'm just gonna take these

empty barrels down to the lake," he called down from his seat. "I only got about enough oil left in my tank to make it there."

"I don't care what your reason is," Anvil said, keeping the rifle pointed at Gus. "You're trespassing. So turn around and get back onto the No. 4!"

"You wouldn't shoot a man just for trespassin', would you?"

"I'm not going to shoot *you!"* Anvil called back. "I'm just going to blow a hole through the engine of your machine, that's all!"

"You wouldn't dare!"

"There's only one way to find out if I dare. Just come another inch this way and you'll know!"

In his own mind Jerry was convinced Anvil would do exactly what he said. Gus apparently believed so too, because he uttered an oath, then opened the throttle of the tractor, heading the machine for the No. 4 claim. Then he got down and came over to the borderline between the claims. "Come on over here, Anvil," he called. "Maybe we can come to some kind of an agreement. No use flyin' off the handle and givin' each other all this trouble, seein' as how we're neighbors."

"Some neighbor!" Jerry remarked.

"Well, let's hear what he wants," Anvil said. They approached the boundary line warily and stopped a dozen feet from Gus. "What you got up your sleeve now?" Anvil demanded.

"What's it worth to you to let me go down and

bring a load of oil back up here?" Gus took a roll of bills out of his pocket.

Anvil eyed the money but only for a moment. "If that whole glacier was solid gold and you owned it all, lock, stock and barrel, it wouldn't be enough to bribe me, Gus Kramer. You can put that in your pipe and smoke it!"

Jerry admired the honesty and courage of the white-haired little sourdough. Here was a man he knew his dad would like.

"That's right honorable of you," Gus said sarcastically. "Where's Ed gone, anyway?"

"To get the marshal."

"He'd better be awful sure of himself, or I'll sue him for false arrest."

"Don't worry, he went to Anchorage to see a lawyer first."

"Oh, so he's gone to see a lawyer, has he?"

"That's right."

"Well, that's his privilege, but he's wastin' his time and money. I happen to know a pretty good lawyer myself and he already told me I got nothin' to worry about."

"We'll see about that." Jerry sounded confident.

Gus turned on him. "It don't think I was talkin' to you, punk."

"Well, I—" Jerry stammered.

"You act like a big shot—who are you, anyway?"

"That's none of your business," Jerry flared back at him.

"Then keep your trap shut after this when grown-ups

are talkin'." Gus glared at him. "I know who you are, all right—you're just another cheechawker tryin' to make like a tough Alaskan." He turned back to Anvil. "How about access rights? What's he gonna do about that? You guys have to give me a way in and out of my claim."

"Only when there's an agreement," Anvil said. "You should have thought of that before you got yourself all sewed up, Gus. That's no worry of ours."

"I've got a right to get out of here to go see a lawyer about access rights."

"Well—"

"All I ask is for you to let me hike across so I can get to my boat down at the lake."

"I won't deny you that, but I'm not giving you the right to come back. Once you go out, you're out!"

"I'll worry about gettin' back when the time comes." Gus turned around and went to his tent. A few minutes later he returned carrying a packsack and a rifle. Anvil kept his own gun at the ready just in case the big man might try something. But Gus went past them without a word and headed toward the lake at a fast walk.

When Gus was well on his way they went back into the wanigan and Anvil stood his rifle in a corner. "Well, I guess it takes all kinds to make a world," he said as he started dishing up the meal, "but when you run into a guy like him it makes you wonder why his kind are necessary."

"I never saw anyone as mean as he is in my life," Jerry said.

"And neither did I." Anvil thought for a moment

then said gently, "But maybe you shouldn't have interrupted when we were talking, lad."

"I—I guess maybe I shouldn't have," Jerry said, turning red with embarrassment. There it was again. Won't I ever learn, he thought.

"It doesn't make any difference to me," Anvil said, "but lots of older fellows think young lads like yourself should be seen and not heard—and maybe they're right."

"I—I'll try to remember that." Jerry looked down, trying to hide his humiliation.

"Well, I've said my piece so let's forget about it," Anvil said cheerily. "What do you say we wrap ourselves around a bite of supper? And try to forget about Gus, too, or you might spoil your appetite."

"It's kind of hard to forget the way he slapped you down out there this morning," Jerry said, as he sat down at the table. "I don't see how you kept from shooting him when you had the drop on him a little while ago."

Anvil set a plate of pork and beans in front of Jerry and took the biscuits out of the oven. "There was a time I just might have been tempted to do it—" he shook his head slowly. "But whenever I get some silly notion like that in my head I stop and think about one time back in the Gold Rush when the boys caught a young fellow stealing a sack of flour in one of the camps up on the Yukon. Now in those days a sack of flour might mean the difference between life and death to a man out on the trail and somebody yelled, 'String him up!' and they did and I stood by in the crowd and watched them do it . . . and at the time it seemed like a pretty good idea. But since then I've been hungry enough at times to have stolen a sack of flour myself if I could have gotten it. And to this day I can't help thinking of that poor lad. I wish now that I'd tried to stop them from stringing him up." Anvil sat down and looked at the beans and biscuits before him for a moment, then closed his eyes. He made the sign of the cross and said something in a low voice. Then he began to eat.

When they had finished Jerry said, "Uncle Ed was telling me on the way up here that he wishes he could have lived in the Gold Rush days, too."

Anvil lighted his pipe before answering. "I'll trade him the years I was there for the years he's got ahead of him any time he wants to. Most of the memories I have of the stampede are of being cold and wet and hungry and tired all the time—and of half-wild, greedy men. In fact there were a lot of guys like Gus Kramer around in those days, yes, sir. And then there was the walking, walking, walking. Always walking, across the swamps and over the mountains, walking from one strike to the next, and always getting there a little too late and always being broke and in debt. We didn't have any gasoline or electricity in those days, either—everything we did, we did with Norwegian steam."

"Norwegian steam—what's that?"

"Sweat and muscles. No airplanes, no trucks, no tractors, no outboard motors. When you moved, you moved on foot. If you took anything along you carried it on your back. The good Lord didn't mean for men to work like we did in those days. No, sir, Jerry, I don't want any part of it. As far as I'm concerned there's no such thing as 'The Good Old Days' and if your Uncle Ed wants them back, he's welcome to them. And as for—" Anvil stopped talking in mid-sentence and sat listening intently. "Did you hear a shot, Jerry?"

"I thought I heard something." Jerry jumped up.

The echo of two more gunshots came rolling across the glacier flats as Anvil opened the door. "They're coming from the direction of Tustumena Lake," he told Jerry. "Now what do you suppose that fool is blazing away at down there?"

"Do you think it's Gus shooting?"

"He's probably getting in a little target practice. And he'll need it if he thinks he's going to shoot his way back onto Ed's No. 4."

"You don't think he'd do anything like that, do you?"

"From the way he acted around here today, nothing would surprise me any more." Anvil undressed and got into his bunk. "Well, don't let it keep you awake, lad. Get a good night's rest because I'm going to work the pants off you tomorrow."

Jerry got into his bunk, but instead of dropping off to sleep, he lay listening to the water rushing along in Glacier Creek, thinking how unbelievable the whole situation was. If he were to write his friends back home and tell them that in one day he had been involved in gunplay, fisticuffs, claim-jumping and a near-drowning, they would think him a liar. Such things didn't even happen in books very often. They were too unrealistic. But wasn't Alaska itself an unrealistic land? The climate, the setting, the people—were unlike any Jerry had ever known Outside. But before he fell asleep he asked himself once more, "Is this all happening to me?"

Jerry ached all over when Anvil wakened him in the morning. When they had finished breakfast, and the dishes were washed and put away, Anvil said, "I think we'll set up the sluice boxes this morning. Then you can start washing gravel while I take the horses and go down to the boat and get the stove oil and the rest of the grub. No need for both of us to spend the day tramping back and forth across the glacier flats when there's gold to be dug."

The sluice boxes were heavy wooden troughs made of two-inch by twelve-inch planks. The horses dragged them into position and Anvil fastened them together so that they formed a gently sloping flume about 200 feet long. Running from east to west, they were parallel to the high gravel bank that lay roughly along the boundary between the No. 3 and No. 4 claims. They put the highest section of the flume into place last so that the sluice box protruded out into Glacier Creek. Immediately water began to race along through the boxes, discharging at the far end and running off across the flats in one of the dried-up creek beds. When the water was flowing properly Anvil pointed into the flume. "See how the riffles slow the water down, Jerry," he said, indicating the crosspieces nailed into the bottom of the sluice boxes. "We've got the water running just fast enough to carry the dirt and gravel away. But the gold is heavier, and will sink and stick behind the riffles. Hand me that muck stick and I'll show you how we do it."

"The what?" Jerry looked puzzled.

"The muck stick—shovel, I mean."

Jerry handed him the long-handled shovel and Anvil began digging into the bank and pitching gravel into the sluice box. "We won't hit much color here," he said, "but all this overburden has to come off so we can get at the pay dirt underneath. You never can tell where you'll find a pocket of gold so we wash everything we stick a shovel into. Start at this end of the flume up here by the creek and work toward the far end. Try not to throw too much dirt in at once, though, or you'll clog her up. And don't put in any big rocks because you'll just have to take them out again."

"When do we take the gold out?"

"Oh, don't worry about the gold for a while. We'll shut the water off one of these days and see how we're making out." Anvil gave the shovel back to Jerry and stood by and watched him work for a few minutes.

"You're not getting the swing of it. Here, I'll show you again." Anvil reached for the shovel.

Jerry's chin came out. He was reluctant to hand the tool over. Didn't these people up here think he could do anything without being told how to do it? They seemed to have the idea if you didn't do everything their way, you were a hundred per cent wrong.

Anvil seemed to be reading his mind. "I only want to make it easier for you, lad. You were going at it too hard. You've got to let the shovel do most of the work."

Jerry gave him the shovel and watched while Anvil made a few effortless swinging motions of his body. He handed the shovel back, and Jerry tried to emulate the movement Anvil had made. After a few swings the old man said, "You're getting it now, but you don't need to work so fast. I don't think you'll run out of work for a day or two."

Jerry looked up at the millions of tons of gravel before him. Then he went to work.

Anvil put the pack saddles on the horses and headed across the rocky flats toward the lake. When the old man was well on his way Jerry said to himself, "To heck with you, Mister. This I'm going to do my own darn way." He went back to shoveling the way he'd done in the beginning, short stabs at the gravel heap, the dirt lifted and thrown by the sheer strength of his muscles. His way was faster, he thought, because the shovel didn't have to travel so far. But before long the sweat was pouring from him, his arms and shoulders began to ache; his palms were getting raw and his knees trembled. Man, this *was* hard work! He sat down and rested for a while and when he went to work again his muscles would not function. He switched over and tried Anvil's way again. Despite the aches and pains the dirt flew effortlessly. "Hm," he said to himself, "maybe he's got something after all."

As Jerry perfected the technique Anvil had shown him, he discovered that pitching gravel into the sluice boxes wasn't especially hard. But it did keep him sweating. He stopped shoveling to take off his shirt. The sun felt good on his skin, and while he rested he wondered how much gold had accumulated in the riffles since he'd begun working. It was simple enough to find out. All he had to do was stop the flow of water through the flume and look. He went to the upper end of the flume and lifted the sluice box out of the creek. When the water had drained away he came back and looked in. All he could find in the wet box were a few rocks that had been caught in the riffles, nothing else.

Disappointed at finding no gold, Jerry sat down on the sun-warmed gravel bank beside the flume. He had lost all incentive to work. He didn't mind working and working hard if he could see some return for his efforts. But since his earnings depended entirely upon the amount of gold that came out of the sluice box, it was downright discouraging to shovel as much gravel as he had this morning and have nothing at all to show for it—not so much as a speck of gold dust. It was just like working for nothing, and he could have done better washing dishes. At least then he'd been sure of having something in his pay envelope at the end of the week. Once again he began to wonder what kind of a deal he'd gotten himself into. Well, at least his uncle had warned him that mining was a gamble.

He looked around at the acres of gravel. Anvil had said all this overburden had to come off to get at the pay dirt that lay underneath. But why didn't they have a tractor to remove the barren, worthless stuff? That was the only way to make money in this game—do it with machinery. Maybe Gus Kramer was as crooked as a snake but at least he knew the value of power. No, sir, Jerry couldn't understand why his uncle did everything by hand, not when there were tractors to be had. Now there was something he wouldn't mind doing at all, driving one of those big diesel cats.

A swarm of mosquitoes came out of nowhere and began biting at him. They tiptoed maddeningly across his bare skin. He tried to ignore them but finally in self-defense he had to get up and put his shirt back on. Then he put the end of the sluice box in place and when the water from Glacier Creek was again rushing through the flume he came back and took up the shovel once more. It seemed like an awful waste of time, though, moving those tons and tons of gravel with a shovel that held no more than ten pounds at a time. But he guessed it had to be done.

Jerry heaved a dozen or so scoops into the flume then stopped to wipe the mosquitoes off his sweaty forehead. Maybe this was necessary work but why was he the one that had to do it. It was tough being the low man on the totem pole.

He shoveled a bit more, then stopped again. How much dirt had he moved so far this morning—a ton, two tons, ten? Why you could shovel a thousand tons here and the place wouldn't look any different. What the heck, he bet he could sit down here and not do another lick all day and nobody would ever know the difference. Jerry tossed the shovel aside and started for the wanigan.

But what would Anvil say if he came back and found him not on the job? Well, he could see the old man coming across the flats while he was still a long way off and he could get back to the shovel before Anvil got here.

Then he remembered something else. Back home his dad had said something about facing up to his responsibilities. Well, he guessed this was what he meant. He had been accepted as a man and given a man's job to do. And he was trusted to get it done without any supervision. Anvil didn't need a foreman to watch over him to see that he did what he had to do. Nor did his uncle. This was a part of the game and the pay of all depended on how much gravel he, Jerry Nelson, put through the sluices. Maybe he hadn't turned up any gold so far this morning—but perhaps in the next shovelful he would.

He went back and picked up the "muck stick" and the scoopfuls of gravel flew faster and faster. A dollar in that one, he said to himself, and a dollar in that one, and a dollar in that one. Before long he had picked up the swing of it again and the thought of the nuggets and gold dust underfoot spurred him on. This might be the year of the big strike, and the quicker the overburden was removed the sooner they would get to it. The sweat began to run down his face but Jerry was glad he hadn't walked off the job—in spite of his sore hands and aching back.

Anvil had been gone about an hour when Jerry heard a clattering off to his right. Horses were coming from the direction of Tustumena Lake, running at a full gallop with manes and tails streaming out behind! As they drew near he saw the pack saddles were still empty and the lead ropes were dragging. He dropped his shovel and ran forward, yelling and waving his arms so as to turn the runaway horses before they could reach Gus Kramer's ditch. The Kashooks, aroused by his shouts, came out of their tent and ran to help stop the horses.

But the animals had run themselves out and when they reached familiar ground they slowed of their own accord. When they got to the wanigan they stood snorting and breathing heavily, their flanks covered with a lather of sweat. Jerry caught one by its halter rope and Mike Kashook caught the other. While they stood patting and talking to the horses, the terror-stricken animals kept looking back toward the lake with fear in their red-rimmed eyes. "Somethin's sure scared these fellas," the Indian said.

"Do you suppose anything has happened to Anvil?" Jerry asked.

Mike shrugged. "Hard tellin'."

"I think I'd better go and see if he's all right. Would you take care of the horses?"

"Sure, kid, I'll take care of 'em," Mike said, "but if I was you I'd carry my gun along. Never can tell what you might run into."

## CHAPTER X

When Jerry came out of the thickets onto the shore of Tustumena Lake, he saw that the sand underfoot was scuffled up over a large area. It looked as though a violent football game had been played there, a game in which at least one of the players had been a long-toenailed individual who had left broad tracks.

Then he stopped short. Just a few yards ahead, a man was lying, face up. Almost unrecognizable now because of the blood that covered his head and face, Jerry knew it was Anvil Bergen. The old man's clothes were ripped almost off and one leg was askew and obviously broken. A short distance away his Winchester rifle lay half-buried in the sand. At first Jerry thought the man was dead and was afraid to come any nearer. He'd never seen a corpse and the thought that this might be one terrified him. While he was trying to make up his mind whether to run away or stick around he heard a groan. Anvil wasn't dead! He hurried forward and as he knelt beside the badly injured man he heard the groan again and saw Anvil's chest rising and falling. He was breathing painfully. "Anvil," he said, "it's Jerry; can you hear me?"

The injured man opened his eyes a crack and asked feebly, "Who?"

"Jerry—Jerry Nelson."

"Jerry Nelson?" He closed his eyes and lay for a moment in silence. "Oh, it's you, Jerry." His voice was hardly more than a whisper. "What are you doing here?"

"The horses came back to the wanigan on the run and I was afraid something might be wrong. What happened?"

Anvil tried to raise himself up on an elbow, then fell back. "Jerry, lad," he said urgently, "did you bring your gun?"

"Yes."

"Jerry, there's a big old wounded brownie back there in the thicket somewhere and you've got to go in and get him."

A wave of fear swept over Jerry at the old man's words. "A what?" he asked, hoping he had not heard right.

"Someone shot up a brown bear . . . and it clawed me. I didn't have a chance."

"We've got to get you to a doctor," Jerry said. He tried to pick Anvil up but the man groaned with pain.

"Leave me alone, Jerry. First you've got to go in and get that brownie. If he ain't killed he'll lay around here and get somebody else."

"Who do you suppose wounded it?" Jerry asked, reaching for the rifle he had laid aside.

"Remember that shooting we heard down this way

after Gus left yesterday; I think that might explain it. You've got to go finish the job."

"Can't I do anything for you first?" Jerry asked.

"Just wash the blood out of my eyes, then set me up against the boat so I can watch you when you go in after him."

Jerry picked Anvil up carefully, carried him to the boat and propped him up in a sitting position with his back against the bow. He dipped his handkerchief into the lake and washed the blood from Anvil's face and eyes. The job almost sickened him. He'd never before seen a person's face in such a condition and had there been someone else around to take charge, he wouldn't have touched him. But something had to be done—so he did it and after the first wave of revulsion he found the job not nearly so bad as he'd feared.

"Now get my gun for me," Anvil said. "I don't know if I can even hold it. But if the bear comes back I don't want to be a sittin' duck."

Jerry got Anvil's rifle and brushed the sand out of the mechanism. He cocked the weapon and laid it in the old man's lap. Anvil noticed Jerry's shaking hands and said, "Get a good hold of yourself, lad. You've got a man's job ahead of you."

"I'm scared to death," Jerry said in a trembling voice.

"You wouldn't be human if you wasn't scared. Now you listen close and do just exactly what I tell you and you won't have anything to worry about. Is your gun loaded and cocked?"

Jerry worked the lever of the Winchester and put a cartridge into the chamber. "What do I do next?"

"Find where the bear's tracks go into the woods and start following them. Go real slow and don't take a step till you're sure he ain't in sight. And don't just keep lookin' straight ahead but look all around. Keep your eyes moving and as soon as you spot him, aim at the end of his nose if he's facing you, and if he's broadside let him have it right behind his front leg. And be sure you don't miss because a sick bear is a lot meaner and harder to kill than a healthy one."

"Well, here goes nothing," Jerry said as he started down the beach looking for the place where the bear had gone into the woods. His mouth was dry and his hands were trembling and sweaty. His knees felt as though they wanted to buckle under him. Inside, his stomach was all a-churn. But this wasn't a new experience for Jerry Nelson, this feeling of fear. Once he'd had to stand and fight a fellow bigger than himself when he would rather have run away. He thought back to that day, a year or so ago, and remembered how scared he'd been then, but all the other guys had been watching and he hadn't dared run. But after the first blow he'd forgotten all about the sensation of fear. He'd fought hard—and he'd been whipped, but no one had ever bothered him again. It had been just like cleaning up Anvil's face—not bad at all once you got at it. But going into a dark, strange forest to kill or be killed by a bear—that was something different. It was not the possibility of being clawed that frightened him so much. It was the actual facing of the wounded animal. But Anvil was watching him, and Anvil was depending on him. And so he had to do it.

When he reached the place where the big footprints of the bear entered the woods, he began walking carefully, one step at a time, toward the tall saplings that stood a short distance back from the shore of the lake. The tangle of light and shadows ahead confused him a little and he didn't know whether he would recognize a bear in there or not. He kept on walking, taking each step with precision so he would not disturb any of the rocks or twigs underfoot. Every few steps he paused and looked around to the right, ahead, to the left, and back again before going on.

Then he was into the woods, moving forward with the gun half to his shoulder, swinging the barrel to left and right. Wherever his eyes looked, that was where the rifle was pointing. A twig crackled somewhere in the underbrush before him and he stopped and stood trembling, trying to pinpoint the source of the sound. He heard a low, coughing grunt close by and more fears than he'd ever known gripped him. He felt an almost overpowering urge to turn and run, to get away from here.

Why should he, Jerry Nelson, fresh from the city and inexperienced, have to be the one to come in here and kill a crazed brown bear? He'd seen brownies in the zoo at home; great, foul-smelling monsters with scimitar-like claws and fearsome fangs, creatures that were terrifying enough to look at through bars and across a moat. And he'd seen what one of them had done to Anvil Bergen who had just been walking along the trail minding his own business. Why should *he* go looking for trouble, Jerry thought? Why couldn't he just fire off a shot or two into the air and then go tell Anvil the job was done? No one would ever know that he hadn't actually killed the bear. And, besides, the injured animal would probably soon die of its wounds, anyway.

But what if it didn't die? What if it waylaid the next person who came along, his uncle, Mike Kashook, some stranger? That was something he'd have to live with for a long, long time. He thought about what Anvil had said about not being able to forget the hungry man who'd been strung up for stealing the sack of flour.

Jerry's hands were trembling, knees shaking and the fearful churning was going on within his stomach. Now which way was it he'd heard that coughing grunt a few minutes before—to the right, the left, or had it been straight ahead? And which way was the lake—behind him? Somehow he'd lost his bearings. Looking upward he could see the sun shining down through the leaves overhead, but that didn't tell him what he wanted to know. He licked his dry lips and peered about him, not daring to move until he was sure which way to go. Suddenly a twig snapped to his left. At the sound, he jumped and turned. A small bird fluttered past his face. He fired a shot at it, then turned and ran in panic—almost running into the brown bear that reared up on its hind legs before him.

The great, shaggy animal seemed confused as it stood there with forepaws dangling in front of its chest, head turning from side to side as it sniffed the air and listened. Jerry stopped dead in his tracks, but strangely his fear had left him. His hands were no longer shaking and his knees were steady. The churning in his stomach stopped. In here among the trees it was hard to judge distance and he wondered how far away the bear was. He was sure it was no more than fifty feet, if that.

He raised the rifle and was about to shoot but remembered that no misses were allowed here. With the bear standing erect, he knew that shooting at the end of the nose was useless, and since it was not broadside to him he could not aim behind the foreleg. Then he must shoot for the heart. Now, which side is the heart on, he thought? The left, of course. But with the bear facing him, its left would be to his right. He was just lining up the sights on the big, yellowish-brown chest, when the brownie gave an angry bellow, came down from its upright stance and charged on all fours through the trees, straight at him!

Jerry lowered the rifle and tried to find the bear's nose over the open sights of the Winchester. There was the big, rippling hump atop the shoulders, then the tips of the rounded ears, the broad forehead, the little, red-rimmed eyes. Somehow it seemed there was no hurry, that he had all the time in the world to do this job. But where was the bear's nose? Ah, there it was, wet and glistening, right over the front sight. Jerry pulled the trigger. BAM! An instant later he heard the heavy mushroom bullet smashing into something solid.

He worked the lever of the rifle, found the bear's

nose again and pulled the trigger once more—BAM! In mid-charge the animal's front legs crumpled under it, the head dropped, and the brownie made a complete somersault before falling flat on its back. He was so close to Jerry that he could have reached out and touched the limp carcass with his foot.

Too busy to think of what might have happened had he missed or tried to run away from the charging brownie, Jerry levered a fresh shell into the chamber. Then he held the muzzle of the gun close to the bear's skull and fired another slug into the brain. He fired once more and the gun was empty. He quickly reloaded and stood back just in case the bear should not yet be dead. When he was sure he walked over to the animal and nudged one of the massive paws with his foot. He shuddered at the length and sharpness of the long, curving claws, still bearing remnants of the clothing it had ripped from Anvil Bergen. He looked into the half-open mouth and marveled that the old man escaped from those ugly yellow fangs alive. He suddenly felt weak and half-sick from the strain he had gone through. He wanted to get far away out into the open. He turned and ran through the trees as though demons might be after him.

"Did you get him?" Anvil whispered when Jerry found his way back to the boat.

"Yes, sir!" Jerry said when he'd gotten his breath back. "I did just what you told me to do and there was nothing to it. But I thought he was going to get *me* for a minute."

"How close did he come before you dropped him?"

"Too close," Jerry said. "About as far as from you to me."

"I was afraid of that," Anvil said weakly. "After you went in there, I wished I hadn't sent you."

"Well, he won't hurt anyone else," Jerry said, proudly. Then, suddenly remembering the old man's injuries, he said, "Now we'd better get you to a doctor."

"There's a hospital at the Army base at Kenai."

"Where is that?"

"A few miles north of Kasilof."

"That will mean going down the river, won't it?"

Anvil nodded.

"How are we going to get through the rapids? You—you can't run the boat now."

"You'll have to do it," Anvil said, "and it's a lot easier than going in after a brownie. You use only one motor going downstream and give her just enough power to steer with. Keep away from the rocks and don't get broadside in the current."

Jerry didn't like the prospect but he decided not to worry about it until he got to the river. Right now there were other things to do. He got Anvil into the boat and pushed it off the beach. Then they went down the lake to the cabin where he got a mattress to put in the bottom for the wounded man to lie on, and blankets to cover him. Then he filled the fuel tanks and got spare cans of gasoline.

The sky was clear, the sun was warm and had it not been for his concern about his companion, Jerry would have enjoyed the run to the west end of Tustumena Lake. There was no wind and the water was calm. The boat ran smoothly, driven along by the two outboard motors. The shoreline quickly fell away behind and the cabin disappeared below the earth's curvature and Tustumena Glacier seemed to pull its great blue tongue back in as they drew away from it. Ahead, looming above the fringe of forest that bordered the lower end of the lake, Jerry could see three great snowy peaks that reared far and above the lesser mountains at their feet. Off to the right, in the northwest, a column of smoke stood far into the sky. Must come from the cooking fires of the people who lived at Kenai village, he decided.

As the trees growing on the western shore became more distinct, Jerry turned left around a point of land; and a short while later found and entered Slackwater. He had stopped only twice to refuel during the two-hour run down the lake. Anvil hadn't said anything for some time and as they sped along between the low, wooded banks Jerry bent forward from the motors and made sure he was all right.

They skimmed past a big rock upon which a beaver had built a house of sticks and mud. A ripple of water was streaming out below and a short distance beyond they passed close by some whirlpools that were eddying near the bank. Then he sensed that the motors were not laboring so hard and noticed that the trees ashore were passing more rapidly. He saw white water ahead and knew he was in the river. His heart was pounding, as he shut one motor off and tilted it forward so that the propeller was out of the water. Idling the other motor, he guided the boat down the center of the channel and into the rapids.

Once into the fast water he was too busy steering to think about his fear. Within minutes the boat had passed through the first series of rapids and was gliding along a winding stretch that flowed deep and swift. He had piloted his uncle's boat through this same section when they'd come up the other day but everything was reversed now, and there was something new around each twist and bend.

Then the boat was swept around a great, sweeping turn called Hong Kong Bend, the place where they had stopped and given Mike Kashook the food and gasoline. Jerry knew that if he was to run into any trouble it would be below here. Already he could hear the roaring of the river ahead. As the current quickened he gripped the tiller tighter and the boat plunged into Silver Salmon Rapids.

After that things happened so fast that most of the obstacles and dangers went by before Jerry recognized them as such. In one stretch the boat rose and fell reminding him of a roller coaster. He took a quick glance over his shoulder and shuddered at the sight of the passage he'd just made. This they must have passed while he'd had his eyes closed in fear on the upstream run.

Then the river twisted to the left and he skirted close to the outer bank to take advantage of the deep water in close to shore. When the channel straightened out again they were out of Silver Salmon. Cabins began to appear now and then in clearings on either bank and he knew the trip was almost over. Yes, sir, he about had this river whipped.

Now to make a landing. Near the highway bridge where he could flag down a passing car would be best. But he came upon it so quickly he was past before he had time to figure out how to safely make the bank. Beyond, the Kasilof ran straight for a distance then was split by a long, narrow wooded island. In the maelstrom where the waters came together again the engine died abruptly. Without power to steer with, the boat began to pivot to the left and in a moment was starting to go broadside in a short, boulder-strewn stretch of rapids. Jerry remembered then that he'd intended to stop and refuel before they got out of Slackwater, but had forgotten. No, the river wasn't whipped yet and he had the impression that it was just beginning to give him a fight.

## CHAPTER XI

"The oars! Where are the oars?" Jerry shouted at himself as the uncontrolled boat entered the rapids and the stern began to swing toward the right. He saw the handles of the oars sticking out from under the mattress Anvil was lying on, but there was no time now to move the injured man to get the oars, for already the boat was broadside to the current.

The boat rocked violently from side to side as it went up the crests and down into the troughs where the water rushed over the tops of sunken rocks. But though the boat seemed in no danger of upsetting here, she would never pass through the narrow opening where the river funneled between two great boulders a hundred yards downstream.

The other motor! The extra motor back there on the stern, the one he had shut off when leaving Slackwater, it must still have gas in it! But could it be started in time to regain control and straighten the boat before it reached the passage between the rocks? Jerry didn't stop to wonder, but flipped the motor upright, slapped the throttle wide open with one hand, and jerked the starter with the other. The motor coughed once, then roared to life. The sudden surge of power drove the boat out of the current directly toward the left hand shore. He twisted the tiller handle violently so as to turn the bow downstream but it was too late. They crashed head-on into the rocks along the bank and came to a jarring stop that splintered the whole front end of the boat. The propeller struck bottom, the pin sheared and the motor ran wild.

Thrown forward by the abrupt stop, Jerry almost landed on top of Anvil. He picked himself up, reached back and shut off the screaming motor. Anvil's broken leg had been twisted by the jolt and he was groaning again. More blood oozed from his bear-chewed shoulder. Jerry tucked the blankets in around him, then he got his rifle from the splintered bow and climbed out onto the bank. Rammed hard ashore and wedged into the rocks as it was, the boat could not drift off again into the river. But just to make sure, he tied the painter to a tree then headed downstream.

Back home running out of gas would have been little more than an inconvenience, but the same thing here on the Kasilof had nearly killed him. Now he knew what Ed meant when he had said things were different in the North. This was one of the things that had to be done right the first time because you might not get a second chance to correct your error. He remembered how Ed had stopped occasionally to check the tanks on the trip up and had left the oars on top of the load so they could be gotten at. He'd been told, but hadn't heeded the instructions. It was the same old story of the spare tire and the tool box. He didn't think he'd ever again forget to check his gas tanks or see that the oars were handy. His carelessness might have meant disaster.

How far would he have to go before he found help, he wondered; a mile, two miles? Jerry knew he could not be too far from his uncle's place on the lower river, but that was over on the opposite shore. And how would he get across? There was only one way to find out and that was to keep going until he got there.

The old Russian boat trail that skirted the river bank was visible here and there in spite of the growth of underbrush. But the bushes were so tangled that Jerry found it easier to travel by going back into the trees, away from the river a short distance. Here the mossy ground made walking easy, but he began having visions of the brownie that had reared up in front of him in the woods back up there on Tustumena Lake. So, assuming the edge of the river to be a less likely place to meet a bear, he came out of the trees and began wading in the shallows close to the bank.

He had been walking for perhaps an hour when he rounded a tight bend of the river and heard the sound of outboard motors running in unison. A few minutes later a big white boat came around the bend, traveling high and light and fast. He recognized his uncle sitting in the stern, and as the boat drew near he began waving his arms and shouting. His uncle looked his way then abruptly changed course and headed for shore.

"My gosh," he said as Jerry came down over the

bank and jumped into the boat, "what in the world are you doing down here on the lower river?"

Jerry told him the story from the beginning.

"You mean to tell me you went into the woods all by yourself and blasted down a wounded brown bear?"

"Yes."

"And then you shot the river by yourself?"

"But I wrecked the boat, Uncle Ed. I should have remembered the gas and I should have thought about the oars."

"Well, it's done so let's forget about it. You say Anvil is still up there in the boat? We'd better hurry."

"If it's not too late."

Jerry pushed the boat away from shore and Ed started the motors. They went roaring up the river and the empty boat seemed to fly over the rapids instead of laboring sluggishly against the current as it had when they'd gone up before. They reached the place below the island where Anvil's boat was tied.

Ed eased in close to the wrecked craft and they lifted the mattress with Anvil on it into Ed's boat. At the landing near Ed's winter cabin, Jerry helped his uncle carry the injured man into the back of the truck, and within an hour they had him in the Army hospital near Kenai village.

Jerry was almost sickened again when Anvil's bloody clothing was removed and he saw the wounds the old man had suffered. But he stayed with his uncle in the emergency room while the doctor cleansed and probed the injuries. "How is he?" Ed asked when the surgeon had finished his preliminary examination.

"To be frank with you he's in pretty bad shape, but from what I've seen of some of the other old-timers up here, I'd say he'll make it all right—with a little luck. We've got a lot of sewing to do on him and a couple or three bones to set. Just offhand I'd say if we can control the infection, he'll make it, but a bear bite is a cinch to give us trouble."

"If anyone can pull through he will," Ed said, "but just between you and me, Doc, it will take a lot more than a brownie to do Anvil in."

"Anvil? Well named, isn't he?"

"He's as tough as they come."

"Tell me," the surgeon said as he prepared to go back to work, "just what is it that makes you people live out there in the back country with all those dangerous animals running around loose? If you've got to live out there, why don't you kill off all the bears and be done with it? I'm getting tired of having to stitch somebody back together every couple of months."

"Do you ever get any automobile accident cases dumped in your lap here, Doc?" Ed asked.

"Oh, two or three a week."

"And you're complaining about the bears?"

Ed reached for his hat. "I've always said the brownies were here first and any time we go fooling around out in their bailiwick we're looking for trouble. So don't blame the bears when one of us gets chewed up a bit. I'll bet you'd be an ornery customer yourself if you caught some strange character prowling around in your house."

"You can say that again."

Since finding Anvil on the lake shore this morning Jerry had agreed with the doctor—kill off all the bears. But after listening to his uncle he began to see things from the animals' point of view.

Ed continued. "All the brownies want is to be left alone and most of them *will* leave you alone if you give them half a chance." He put his hat on. "I don't suppose there's anything more we can do, is there?"

"No, I'm afraid not," the doctor said. "We'll do everything we can for your friend and what's to happen, will happen. Just be thankful you got him here when you did. A few more hours and we couldn't have done a thing for him."

"When he comes to, tell him we had to go back up to the lake to take care of some unfinished business. I'll be down in a day or two to see how he's making out."

## CHAPTER XII

Ed catnapped in the bottom of the speeding boat, and Jerry steered toward the glacier at the upper end of Tustumena Lake. The surface of the water looked like a sheet of polished steel. He had not yet accustomed himself to the bright Alaskan nights and he found it hard to believe that it was midnight, so clearly and distinctly did the features of the landscape stand out in the weird light. At this time of year, here close beside the 60th degree of North Latitude, the sun dipped but briefly behind the northern horizon before rising again to take another great, circling sweep around the sky.

After he had passed the roiling mouth of Glacier Creek, Jerry turned and headed toward shore at full speed. When the bow was near the beach he cut the motors and the boat ran almost its full length up onto the sand. Ed awakened and sat up as the dory grounded. "Getting to be an expert, aren't you?" he said, grinning.

"That's the way you did it when we came up here before," Jerry said.

"It's all right to land hard and fast as long as you know what kind of beach you're going onto, otherwise you might tear the bottom out of your boat."

They got out and pulled the boat the rest of the way up out of the water and tied it fast to a tree. "Now," Ed said, picking up his rifle, "the first thing I want to do is to have a look at that brownie you killed this morning. By looking at the bullet holes we just might find out what kind of a rifle it was wounded with before it got Anvil. Do you think you can find it again?"

"That's one place I'll *never* forget," Jerry said, taking his gun out of the boat.

The tracks the brown bear had made still showed in the sand and when Ed stopped and looked down at them he gave a low whistle. "Man, you really tangled with a lollapalooza!" he said. "I'll bet he'll go over half a ton. Where do we go from here?"

Jerry led the way.

When they came to the place where Gus Kramer's shovelnose was stranded on the beach at the water's edge Ed stopped and felt the motors. "Still warm," he said. "Gus can't have gotten here more than 15 or 20 minutes ago. Did you see any sign of him while we were coming up the lake?"

"Gosh, I didn't notice," Jerry said, "but I was looking at the glacier most of the time for the last hour or so."

"It would be hard to see that yellow boat against the beach in this light, anyway," Ed said. He counted the barrels that were in the boat, ". . . . seven, eight, nine, ten. Ten barrels at 55 gallons apiece. He's got enough oil here now to keep that cat working for quite a spell."

"When he tried to drive across the claim yesterday he said he only had about enough left to get him down here to the lake for more, so I guess he was getting pretty low."

Ed stood looking at the barrels. "One thing's for sure," he said after a moment. "That machine will be worthless if he can't get fuel to it. Maybe we'd better forget the brownie for now and hotfoot it up to the claim just in case he does try to come out. As long as we can keep that tractor pinned down on the No. 4 we've got a weapon to fight him with."

The northern sky was brightening as they left the lake and Jerry could hear the twittering of awakening birds that had spent the brief twilight roosting in the saplings. It made him think of the robins he had heard in the cherry tree before daybreak the morning they had left home. He thought about his parents and felt a pang of homesickness.

They were halfway across the flats when, with no warning at all, a gust of wind hit them in the face. Up ahead a great cloud of dust began swirling down off the icefield. "Williwaw!" Ed shouted as they bent their heads into the sudden gale. "It's a good thing we got off the lake when we did."

"Where is all the dust coming from?" Jerry asked as they hurried along.

"Off the ice. That's rock flour, rock that's been ground to powder by the glacier. Dustiest place in the world, out here on the flats when the wind blows. Let's step on it—if it gets much worse we'll have to stop and sit it out."

Stumbling and tripping over rocks, and choking and coughing as the dry, powdery rock dust got into their lungs, they trotted the last quarter mile. Even after they reached the shelter of the wanigan Jerry did not feel secure, for it shook fiercely with each violent gust of wind. Ed pointed out the window toward the two tents just visible through the dust. "Consider yourself lucky we're not holed up in one of those things," he said. The way the tents were flapping, Jerry expected at any moment to see the frail canvas shelters go sailing off.

After an hour the wind began to die, the wanigan rocked less violently, then the newly-risen sun appeared—a dim, yellow-red disk shining faintly through the haze. As suddenly as it had started, the williwaw died away and the last of the dust went swirling away to settle on the flats.

A brief silence followed the storm; then Jerry heard the tractor roaring to life over beyond the tents on the No. 4 claim. "Well," Ed said, "there comes Gus now and I'll bet he doesn't know we're within miles of here. Let's go surprise him."

Jerry and his uncle were waiting on the boundary between the claims when the tractor crawled up over the top of the gravel heap. Gus Kramer's mouth dropped open when he saw them. He stopped the tractor and got down. "All right, Carlson," he said in a sarcastic tone, "I suppose you're gonna be big-hearted, too, and tell me I can't come across, either."

"That's right."

"What'd they tell you up at Anchorage?"

In all the excitement Jerry had completely forgotten the purpose of his uncle's trip to the city and he listened intently to what Ed was saying. "It will have to go to trial," he explained, "to find out whether the assessment work I've done on my first three claims will count as work that will benefit those that are covered by ice."

"I'll see you in court then." Gus started back toward the tractor.

"Just a minute, Gus," Ed called after him.

The big man stopped and looked back. "Yeah?"

"Until the case is settled no work can be done on the No. 4—by either of us."

"Who says so?"

Ed reached into his pocket and took out a paper. "I've got a copy of the restraining order here that was issued by the Federal Court. Want to see it?"

"I won't touch that paper. Until I been legally served I ain't bound by nothin'. I know a little about the law myself."

"I'm not trying to serve any paper on you, Gus. A deputy United States marshal is going to fly down here sometime today and he'll serve it on you."

"Well, I ain't been served yet and as far as I'm concerned this is still my claim and I'm gonna keep on workin' it."

"That's up to you, Gus, and I'll sure appreciate any improvements you make on the property."

Gus spat. "I'm gonna make some improvements, all right, but they won't be for your benefit; no, sir." He climbed back onto the tractor and put it in gear. "I got just about enough oil left to do what I want to do." He started the tractor with a jerk, spun it around and headed back down over the bank. The blade lowered and began to carry great scoops of gravel into the swiftly flowing water of the ditch.

"What do you suppose he's doing that for?" Jerry commented.

"It looks like he's damming up the ditch," Ed said.

"If he does, Glacier Creek will go dry, won't it?"

"It sure will. Let's stick around and see what he's up to."

Within half an hour Gus had made a dam that reached from the top of the gravel ridge to the face of the ice. With its outlet blocked, the water ceased to flow and began to rise within its confines, forming a narrow pond along the foot of the glacier. Gus spread a layer of dirt and gravel along the top of the fill and was coming back in reverse when the tractor's engine sputtered. The big machine came to a stop in the middle of the dam.

"Sounds like his tank has finally run dry," Ed said. They watched Gus trying to start the engine again. "I'm sure glad that's not my cat out there."

"Why?" Jerry asked.

"Look. You can see the water rising behind the fill already and when it gets a few feet higher that dam is just going to dissolve. Once the water breaks through it will be goodbye tractor."

"Well, it's his tractor and he put it there. I'm not going to worry any about it."

"And neither am I," Ed said. "Hey! What's he up to now?"

Gus climbed down from the tractor, got a shovel and

a bucket, then disappeared down over the bank below the dam.

"What do you think he's going to do with the bucket and shovel?" Jerry asked.

"That must be why he built the dam, so he can go down into the creek bed and make his cleanup before the marshal gets here—he thinks."

"I wonder what he'll do when he finds out all the gold has washed down onto the No. 3 claim?"

"That should be interesting."

Red-faced with rage, Gus looked up from the bottom of the dried-up ditch and shook his fist at Jerry and Ed. "Somebody's cleaned out all my dust and I think I know who did it!"

"From under ten feet of fast water?" Ed called down to the man standing on the solid rock of the stream bed. "Don't be silly."

"I don't know how it was done but when I find out somebody's gonna pay through the nose!"

"You don't think we did it, do you, Gus?"

"I ain't sayin' you did and I ain't sayin' you didn't, but I wouldn't put it past you!"

Ed looked down into the empty channel. "I'll be honest with you, Gus. We've got the gold all right, but you gave it to us!"

"Meanin' what?"

"You should have learned a little more about hydraulic mining before you dug that ditch. You had about ten times the amount of water you needed and it was running so fast it washed everything down onto my No. 3 claim."

Gus stood glowering for a moment then flung his bucket and shovel clanging down onto the naked bedrock. "It's still my gold and I'm gonna get it back!"

Ed shook his head and grinned down at Gus. "Don't you remember the old proverbs; gold is where you find it and finders keepers, losers weepers?"

"Keep your proverbs. This is a matter for the law."

"And possession is nine points of the law—that's another proverb, if I remember right."

"I ain't gonna waste my time arguin'," Gus raged as he climbed out of the stream bed. "I got more important things to do."

"Such as getting your cat onto solid ground before the dam washes out?"

Gus looked toward the tractor. Already bits of dirt and gravel were loosening and slipping off into the rising water behind the fill. "Blast you to pieces, Ed Carlson, if you'd have let me go get some oil this wouldn't of happened!"

"Let's be reasonable, Gus," Ed said. "You started all this no-trespassing business when you sent Mike Kashook with a loaded gun to keep me off my own claim. What do you expect me to do, welcome you with open arms? Two can play this game, you know."

Gus stood gritting his teeth and clenching his fists for a moment. Then he relaxed and said in a low, calm voice, "All right, Ed, I guess I have been pretty much of a snake about the whole deal and I'm sorry about it. We're actin' like a couple of kids, bein' at each other's throats like this. What do you say we shake hands and forget about it?"

Ed looked at the grimy hand Gus held out then shook his head. "It's hard to forget some of the deals you've pulled."

"Now look, Ed, you know as well as I do that you've got to be tough to get anywhere in this world. If you don't take what you can get somebody else'll beat you to it."

"Does that include jumping homesteads?"

"If Anvil had any legal right to be there, Uncle Sam wouldn't have backed me up—it was all done legal accordin' to the law."

"Just a bit *too* legal to suit me," Ed said.

"All right, Ed, all right," Gus said. "You don't like me, so that's that. But I've got to get my cat off that fill before she washes out. Everything I got is tied up in that machine and all I'm askin' is that you let me bring just five gallons of diesel oil across your claim."

"It will take you two hours to go to the lake and bring a can of oil back here and that fill won't last half an hour—if that."

"Let me use one of your horses," Gus begged.

"You couldn't get there and back on a horse even if I'd let you—and I won't."

"What am I gonna do then? I got to do somethin'."

The water had risen to within three feet of the top of the fill and already the tractor was starting to lean a bit as the sodden ground settled. Jerry was surprised when his uncle said, "What will you take for her—as is, where is?"

"That machine is worth a good fifteen thousand dollars."

"And it won't be worth fifteen cents by the time that fill caves in. You'd better hurry and make up your mind, Gus, because if that machine settles much more I won't give you a nickel for it."

"What'll you give me?"

"It's worth one hundred dollars to me and not a cent more." Ed reached inside his shirt and took some bills out of his money belt. "One hundred bucks—take it or leave it."

Gus looked at the money then at the tractor. "How you gonna get her out of there?" He wiped the sweat from his forehead.

"It's going to cost you the cat to find out."

"I'll tell you what I'll do," Gus said frantically. "I'll give *you* a thousand bucks if you'll tell me how you'd get her off."

"With sky hooks, how else could I do it?" Ed started to put his money away. "All right, Gus, if you don't want to do business that's up to you. Come on, Jerry, let's go back to the wanigan and fix us a bite to eat. I'm as hungry as a bear."

"So am I," Jerry said, "a *brown* bear."

"Now, hold on a minute," Gus pleaded. "You've got me over a barrel. A hundred bucks is a hundred bucks. I'll take it."

Ed turned to Jerry. "Run down to the wanigan and get the writing pad and the fountain pen that's on the shelf over the table. I want a bill of sale on this deal."

As Jerry hurried to the wanigan he couldn't help thinking that his uncle must be out of his mind to pay even as little as a hundred dollars for Gus Kramer's tractor. He must have something up his sleeve, though, but for the life of him Jerry couldn't figure out how the tractor could possibly be saved.

When he got back Ed took the writing materials and handed them to Gus.

"The end of that barrel will make a good desk."

"What'll I put on here, anyway?"

"Oh, the date and 'Tustumena Glacier, Alaska.' And then, 'I, Gus Kramer, do hereby transfer all title to tractor, make and model such-and-such, to Edward M. Carlson, for the sum of one hundred dollars.' Then sign it."

When Gus had filled out the paper Ed called Mike and Anna Kashook from their tent to sign their names as witnesses. Then he counted the hundred dollars and handed it to Gus. "Is it all there?"

Gus counted the money again. "All here."

Ed folded the bill of sale and put it into the pocket of his jacket. "Jerry, run down to the wanigan again and bring me a couple of cans of stove oil, will you? And hurry!"

Gus swallowed hard. "Stove oil?"

"Sure," Ed said. "When I buy stove oil they quite often take it out of the same tank as they do the diesel oil. Didn't you know that, Gus?"

Gus pounded himself on the forehead with his fist. "Stove oil! And I've got a whole barrel of the stuff over by my tent right now. Stove oil! Why didn't *I* think of that!" he raged.

Yes, sir, Jerry thought as he raced off to get the oil, a fellow didn't mind taking orders from a guy who knew exactly what he was doing. Why even Gus Kramer, an old experienced tractor operator, hadn't known that stove oil would work in a diesel engine! But his uncle had. Yes, sir, he was proud to be the nephew of Ed Carlson.

## CHAPTER XIII

As soon as he had poured the stove oil into the tractor's fuel tank, Ed pushed the starter and the big diesel came to life. Jerry stood on the solid ground watching, afraid the fill would wash out any moment. He held his breath while his uncle cautiously let in the clutch, slipped the tractor into gear, then began backing carefully along the top of the dam. Ed was almost off when the right side of the tractor began to tilt toward the water. The ground began dissolving beneath the tracks and for an instant the ponderous machine teetered. Then he jerked the throttle wide open and the tractor backed out onto firm ground, only a moment before the water started to trickle over the top. Ed didn't stop the tractor until it was across the boundary and onto the No. 3 claim.
"Pretty foxy, ain't you?" Gus Kramer said.

"You just outsmarted yourself, Gus."

"All right, so I outsmarted myself."

It was something, Jerry gloated, to hear Gus admitting he'd been outwitted. It was a pleasure to see a guy like that taken down a peg or two!

"I'll tell you what I'll do, Ed," Gus continued. "I'll give you back your hundred and another thousand, too, if you'll tear up that bill of sale."

Ed reached over and patted the side of the tractor. "Thanks, Gus, but I'm going to keep this baby."

"Let's do this then: on top of the thousand, I'll get off the No. 4, once and for all, if you'll let me have her back. And it'll save us both a lot of time and money fightin' it out in court."

Jerry's uncle shook his head. "It's no use talking, Gus. You started all this and now I'm going to see it through to the end. But if you want to make a deal, how much will you take for the oil you've got down there in your boat?"

"I just might be needin' that oil. It ain't for sale."

"O.K., that's your business, but if you should change your mind I'll take it off your hands."

"I wouldn't sell you a teacup of that oil if I was—" Gus's voice was drowned out by a sudden roaring sound overhead. Jerry looked up just as a yellow helicopter slipped in over the canyon wall and settled to earth a short distance away. When the engine was still and the rotor had stopped spinning, the door opened and a man stepped out—a man with a badge on his shirt and a pistol in his holster.

The officer stood looking toward the tractor for a moment. "Which one of you is Gus Kramer?" he asked. He was close enough for Jerry to read the words on his badge, "Deputy U. S. Marshal."

They all looked toward Gus and the big man said, "I'm Kramer."

The deputy took a paper out of his pocket. "I have an order issued by the Federal Court for the Second Judicial District in Anchorage restraining you from doing work of any nature on Carlson's Discovery Claim No. 4 until authorized to do so by the court. Do you want me to read it to you?"

"I can read." Gus took the paper and looked it over.

"This order is effective as of now and any violation shall be considered contempt of court."

"I understand." Gus put the paper into his pocket.

"Good," the deputy said, then added, "I'm going back to Anchorage now. Does anyone have anything they'd like me to do up there—any grocery orders, any mail to go out?"

Jerry wished he had a letter ready to send to his folks.

Ed shook his head. "Nothing for me."

"How about you people?" the deputy asked the Kashooks. Mike and his wife shook their heads.

"How about a ride?" Gus asked. "Have you got room for another passenger?"

"You'll have to ask the pilot." The officer wasn't very enthusiastic.

"I can take you to Kenai," the pilot told him. "That's as far as I go, but you can get a bush plane to take you on from there."

"Good enough, Kenai will be fine with me," Gus said. "I'll be with you in a minute." He went to his tent and came out a few minutes later carrying a packsack and climbed into the helicopter.

Mike Kashook began to look worried. "How about me, Gus, what do you want me to do now?"

"Tough luck, Mike. Looks like you're out of a job."

"Ain't we partners like you said?"

"Too bad—no claim, no money." Gus slammed the door shut, the pilot started the engine, the rotor began to whirl and the helicopter soared up from the ground in a cloud of dust. Jerry and the others watched it vanish over the top of the cliff.

Mike Kashook stood looking up into the sky. "He told me I was goin' to make lots of money if I worked for him." His eyes were straining after the helicopter.

"What are you going to do now, Mike?" Ed asked, "go down to the beach and do some fishing?"

"Too late to go fishin'. All the locations are full up by now. I don't know what to do."

"Well, now that I've got a tractor I can move enough dirt to make it worth while to hire some help. How would you like to work for me the rest of the summer?"

Mike grinned. "Good deal."

That sounded good to Jerry, too, now that they had the tractor to push the dirt around. Even though he hadn't done much shoveling he had already had enough of it. And having an extra hand to help out wouldn't hurt any, either.

Ed went on. "And as I recall, Anna's about the best camp cook in this part of the country, isn't she?"

"She sets a good table."

"She can cook for all of us then. I won't be able to pay you much until the season is over but I'll sure make it worth your while after the cleanup."

"Fine, fine." Mike was smiling broadly. "Any way you want it is all right for me, Ed."

"Good. Now the first thing we've got to do is to get enough fuel up here to keep the tractor going for a while. So we'd better take our boats down to Kasilof, then take my truck and go over to Seward and get a load."

"Do you want me to go along, too?" Jerry asked.

"I don't think we've seen the last of Gus so maybe you'd better stick around here and keep an eye on things. Mike and I should be back by tomorrow night."

"Is there anything I should do while you're gone?"

"You can move Mike's tent and stuff off the No. 4 claim and then if you feel like it you better take the fishing pole that's in the wanigan and go down to the lake and catch us a mess of trout."

Jerry shook his head. "If I'm liable to meet any bears down there, I'd just as soon stay here and shovel gravel."

"Well, that's up to you," Ed said. "And speaking of bears, come along and show me that dead brownie. I want to find out what kind of bullet he was wounded with before he jumped Anvil."

"Say," Mike Kashook said, "how we goin' to get that oil up from the lake when we get back with it?"

"We'll take the tractor down now and we can knock a sled together out of saplings and bring the oil barrels back on that."

"Why don't we take that sled of Gus's?"

"No," Ed said, "we won't touch a thing of his."

Ed walked over and looked at the crumbling dam. "I'm surprised that hasn't all washed out by now but I guess with the weight of the tractor off it she's going to last a bit longer than I figured." He studied it a moment or two, then said, "I think I'll just divert some of the water back into the old stream beds so there won't be so much running down Glacier Creek when it does go out." He climbed up onto the tractor seat, started the motor, and drove to the far end of the pond. After he had bulldozed several openings so that the dammed-up stream could again flow down the outlet creeks he put another ten gallons of stove oil into the tank. "Get our guns and climb aboard, Jerry."

Jerry went to the wanigan for the rifles and then got on the tractor behind his uncle and Mike. Glancing down he saw Joe Kashook looking up at them with a long, sad face. "Have we got room for him to come, too?" he shouted above the roar of the diesel engine.

"Sure!" Ed said. He beckoned to Joe and the boy's face broke into a wide grin as he scrambled up into his father's lap. They headed for the lake to the sound of the clattering tracks of the jouncing, lurching tractor.

Just before they reached the water Ed drove deep into the saplings and shut the engine off. "No sense leaving this brute out in the open where everyone can see it. You never can tell who might come along and there's no use asking for trouble." They took their rifles and continued on foot. When they reached the beach Ed said, "All right, Jerry, let's go see that brownie of yours."

Jerry led the way into the thicket, keeping alert and watching in all directions just in case there might be another bear around. When they came to the great, sprawling form of the dead brownie, Ed whistled. "Man, he is a big one! What would you say he'll go, Mike?"

Mike Kashook lifted one of the heavy, stiffened paws and examined the long, sharp claws. "Close to 1,500, I'll bet."

"About as big a bear as I've ever seen, Jerry. No wonder whoever shot it didn't stick around to see if it was dead or not." He walked completely around the bear. "I'll bet you'd like to have a picture taken with him to send back to your folks."

"No, sir." Jerry shook his head vigorously. "If Mom knew I was this close even to a dead bear she'd come up here and drag me home by the ear. No, I'd just as soon forget all about him. I get the jitters every time I think about how he looked when he reared up and came at me."

Ed examined the bear's head. "How many times did you say you shot at him?"

"Twice on the run and then I shot him two more times in the head after he was down."

Ed indicated the wounds in the bear's skull. "One, two, three, four. You might have been scared but it didn't hurt your shooting any." He frowned. "What became of the fifth shot, anyway? Did you decide four shots were enough?"

Jerry reddened. "I'll tell you about it some time."

Working together they tugged at the awkward carcass until it was lying on one side and Ed passed his hands across the thick, foul-smelling hair of the dead animal. "Here's where the bullets went in when he was wounded the first time," he said finally, pointing to three small punctures in the bear's body between the left front and left hind legs. "Now let's turn him over and take a look at the other side."

With great effort they rolled the animal over and found the three bloody splotches where the bullets had come out after passing completely through the bear. "Just as I thought," Ed said, "there's only one kind of a rifle around here with enough power to send a bullet in one side of a brownie and have it come out the other and that's the .30-06."

"You mean an Army rifle?" Jerry asked.

"Yes. Most of the boys up here who have Springfields use mushroom bullets. You know what happens when you hit something with a mushroom bullet, don't you, Jerry?"

"Well, it expands, doesn't it?"

"Right. A mushroom bullet is designed to spread out and blow a great big hole in anything it hits, and it doesn't come out. It stays inside and kills quick and sure. It's a humane bullet. Now, on the other hand, if you shoot a brownie with steel jackets, the slug will hardly even slow him down. A steel-jacketed bullet just goes in one side and comes out the other and about all it does is make the animal sick and awfully mean."

"Like this one?"

"Exactly. A steel jacket is all right for target shooting but nobody in his right mind would ever use them on big game. I wouldn't do it and neither would anyone I know of except—"

"Gus Kramer has got steel jackets," Mike Kashook said.

"Are you sure of that?"

"I seen 'em. He bought a whole box of 'em from one of the soldier boys up at Kenai."

"I know he has a Springfield but I didn't know he was using steel jackets in it."

"Then you're sure it was Gus who wounded the brownie, aren't you?" Jerry asked.

"There's no doubt in my mind, but just try and prove it. He'd never admit it."

They left the dead bear and went back to the beach. Mike and Ed got back in the boats and Jerry and Joe Kashook stood watching until they were far down the lake. Then they headed back toward the glacier.

"Say, Joe," Jerry said to the Indian boy as they neared the sluice boxes on the No. 3 claim, "I wonder why there isn't any water coming out of the lower end of the flume."

"I guess account of the dam maybe, huh?"

"Oh, sure, that's right, no water in Glacier Creek, no water in the flume." He stopped by the empty stream bed where he had been shoveling gravel the day Anvil was hurt. He looked into the sluice box. "Do you know what gold looks like, Joe?" he asked running his finger along the lower edge of a riffle.

"I don't know," Joe said, "but my dad says you're never supposed to look in somebody else's sluice box."

"Why is that?"

"Lookin' at gold makes people crazy. He says as long as you don't look at it it won't bother you none. He says there's more people get in trouble over gold than anything else."

"I'd never heard that before."

"He says guys'll steal gold before they'll touch anything else."

"Maybe that's what's wrong with Gus Kramer," Jerry said.

"Yeah, maybe."

"There's sure nothing in here," Jerry said. "Let's go down in the creek bed and see if we can find any of the gold that Gus washed down from the No. 4 claim."

They walked along the bedrock between the canyon wall and the steep gravel bank. The light was dim, the air bitterly cold. Jerry wondered how long the ice had overlain this place to chill it so. Had the sunlight that shone so bright and warm in the open ever reached into the bottom of this chasm where rushing water and the gouging ice had cut into the solid rock? The sole of his shoe crunched in some sort of sediment that lay in a water-filled depression in the bedrock. He was just bending down to see what it was when he heard Joe say, "Look at the big hole in the rock up there."

"What hole?"

The Indian boy pointed to a dark opening in the left hand canyon wall just ahead.

"By golly, there *is* a hole there! I wonder how far in it goes?" Jerry estimated it to be about four feet wide and not much over five feet in height.

"Sure is dark in there," Joe said, standing on tiptoes so as to see inside.

"Hello!" Joe shouted. After a few seconds they heard an answering echo, "Hello!"

"Boy, it sure took a long time for that echo to come back," Jerry said. He picked up a pebble from the stream bed and threw it as hard as he could. They stood listening to the hollow clatter of the stone as it bounced along the solid rock inside. Joe found a stone for himself and threw it in. "I'll bet it's a half a mile in there!"

"Well, maybe not quite that far, but it's a long way." Jerry stepped back away from the foot of the canyon wall and studied the entranceway that was just about level with his shoulders. "You know, Joe," he said after some thought, "those corners look too square to be natural. I'll bet somebody dug that hole. I wonder if—" He stood thinking for a moment then said, "Do you know what I think, Joe?"

"What?"

"Uncle Ed told me that back in the old days before Alaska belonged to the United States the Russians were supposed to have had a gold mine up here someplace and I'll bet this is it!" Jerry stepped forward again and looked at the lower edge of the opening. "Look, this must be the vein here." He passed his hand over the six-inch-wide strip of yellow-speckled white rock that ran along the floor of the tunnel and vanished into the gloom within. "And look, Joe!" he said, tracing the vein of quartz down the face of the wall to the bedrock and across the stream bed to the gravel bank beyond. "It runs back under Uncle Ed's No. 3 claim! I'll bet you anything this is the lode that he's been looking for!"

"Boost me up," the Indian boy said. "I want to see what's inside." Jerry helped Joe up and he went back into the tunnel a short distance. "Sure is dark in here!" he called out.

"There are a couple of lanterns in the wanigan," Jerry shouted. "Do you want to stay here while I go get them?"

"Sure, I'll stay here!" Joe's voice came echoing out of the darkness.

The bright sunlight hurt Jerry's eyes as he hurried across the flats to the wanigan. He got the lanterns and a box of matches and was starting back when Anna Kashook came out of the tent and called to him. "Where's Joe?"

"He's over at the creek!" Jerry called back.

"Where you goin' with the lanterns?"

"We've found an old tunnel in the canyon wall and we're going to see where it leads!"

"You boys don't stay too long. Dinner is on the stove!"

"When will it be ready?"

"Half an hour!"

"We'll be there!" Jerry called over his shoulder. He trotted off toward the canyon wall, his feet splashing in the two or three inches of water running along the stream bed. When he reached the tunnel Joe was standing in the entrance. He handed up the lanterns and matches and said, "I never lit a lantern in my life, Joe. You'll have to show me how to do it."

When Joe had the lanterns burning he reached down and helped Jerry up, then led the way along the upward-sloping floor of the tunnel. In the dancing yellow light of the lanterns the narrow strip of quartz underfoot gleamed like the center line down the middle of a highway. Joe Kashook was able to walk erect but Jerry had to stoop to keep from hitting his head on the roof.

There was no quartz in the ceiling rock, so he assumed the miners in cutting the tunnel had followed the top of an upward-slanting vein. That accounted for the steep floor underfoot.

Before they had gone fifty feet into the tunnel Jerry was chilled to the bone and his teeth were chattering. Like being dropped into a deep freeze, he thought. Here and there, where underground water had trickled through cracks in the rock, great icicles hung from the walls, glistening like crystal in the lantern light.

As they went deeper and deeper into the heart of the mountain Jerry counted his steps—50, 75, 100 paces he had gone and Joe Kashook was still walking—125 . . . 150. He stopped and looked back toward the faint rectangle of light at the tunnel's door. When he turned around he noticed that the boy's lantern was far-away and no longer bobbing around. Then he heard Joe's voice echoing back. "Hey, Jerry!"

"What is it, Joe?"

"There's some dead guys in here!"

## CHAPTER XIV

"What are you trying to do, Joe, scare me?" Jerry hurried toward the light.

The boy stood aside and pointed toward the face of the tunnel. "I ain't kiddin'—there they are!"

Jerry's pulse leaped, for he recognized the three huddled figures lying on the stone floor for what they were—dead men! A wave of terror passed over him and he fought back an impulse to turn and run, to get out of this tomb-like place. Then he gained control of his nerves again. After all, Joe Kashook didn't seem to be scared and he was only twelve years old. "They're—they're really dead, aren't they?" he asked, hesitantly.

Joe touched one of the bodies with the toe of his shoe. "He's froze as hard as a rock."

Jerry came closer and stood looking down at the dead men. Now that he had lost his fear he wondered why he had been so terrified at first. The men seemed to be only sleeping, one lying on his back with an arm thrown across his forehead, the other two face down. White, almost waxen and perfectly preserved by the intense cold within the tunnel, they could have been carved marble statues. All three were bearded and the hair was shoulder-length. Garbed in rough, canvas-like clothing, they wore heavy boots with wooden soles. The ankles of each man were bound by iron shackles and joined together with a length of chain. He assumed the dead men to have been Russians—but why were they chained?

How had they died and how long had they lain here? Throughout the span of years it took for the ice to march down to the shore of Tustumena Lake and then retreat again? Had they been trapped inside the tunnel and starved? Or had there been an accident? Unanswerable questions leaped to his mind as he stood looking at the three dead miners. So deep in thought was Jerry that he had forgotten he was not alone and jumped, startled, when Joe Kashook said suddenly, "Look at the tools."

There was another mystery. Who could have brought in the hand tools that lay scattered about the tunnel? There were shovels, hammers and drills, all coated with a light film of rust but otherwise intact, apparently preserved by the same cold that had kept the miners looking as they had the day they died. Three lamps of corroded brass, each bearing the stub of a yellow candle, were hung by pointed hooks from crevices in the wall. Jerry struck a match and held it to the wick of one. The flame sputtered then caught and the candle went on burning smokily with a flickering yellow light just as it must have before it had been snuffed out. When—a hundred years ago, or more?

There were holes bored into the tunnel's face, and

from one of them the flattened head of a drill was still protruding. Nearby was a small keg, charred inside and with both ends missing. Not far away Jerry saw a box-like affair on wooden runners, half-filled with broken chunks of the same whitish, yellow-speckled rock that made up the vein down the floor and up the tunnel face. Jerry picked up a chunk of the ore, looked at it by the lantern light, dropped it into his pocket.

Fascinated by all he saw about him, he stood in silence trying to imagine what the men had been doing just before they died. The half-burned candles in the lamps meant they had not been in darkness. That black-bearded fellow there lying face down with his hand just touching the handle of a hammer, what had *he* been doing—driving the drill into the wall? And the other one, also lying on his face, close to the shovel—had he been loading ore for the third, the one with the white hair and whiskers, to drag out to the tunnel mouth in his crude sled?

"What you thinkin' about?" Joe asked.

"I was trying to figure out what killed these people."

"What do you think happened?"

"Well, I can only guess, but—" The candle and the lanterns flickered and Jerry's ears popped as they sometimes did when he was going up or down a steep hill. He thought he heard a rushing sound down toward the entrance to the tunnel. "Did you hear something?" He looked at Joe.

"Yes, and my ears popped," the boy said.

"So did mine."

"I wonder what it was?"

"I don't know. Maybe we'd better go take a look." Keeping his head low so he would not strike the roof Jerry hurried down the sloping floor of the tunnel with Joe right behind him. He was counting his steps and when he reached a hundred expected to see the patch of light that marked the entrance. Everything ahead was black and he heard a gurgling sound. A moment later the light of his lantern reflected back and he found himself ankle-deep in water.

"What's the matter?" Joe asked.

"The end of the tunnel is full of water."

"How did it get there?"

"I'll bet Gus Kramer's dam gave way." Jerry could visualize the torrent of icy water rushing down the stream bed and drowning the tunnel mouth.

"How are we gonna get out of here?"

"We might wait a bit and see if the water goes down."

Joe began to cry. "I don't like it in here and I want to get out."

"I do, too." Jerry said. "But don't worry, Joe—we will." But *could* they? With the entrance flooded it was possible they might never be found. Perhaps this was how the miners had died. Would someone a hundred or a thousand years from now find their bodies, his and Joe's, frozen in this cavern and wonder, too, how and why they had come to be here?

He had never before thought too much about what it meant to die or how it might feel when his time came. Dying and getting killed was something that happened to other people. But now he wasn't so sure. His feet were numb and his hands tingled from the cold. His body shivered and his teeth chattered. What was it like to freeze to death? He'd heard or read someplace of people who'd almost frozen and then been revived. Hadn't they said it was just like drifting off to sleep? That shouldn't be too bad but he still didn't like the idea.

How stupid can you get, he thought. He had known the gravel fill was all set to go out at any time and should have had sense enough not to enter that stream bed, let alone come into the tunnel.

I got myself into this, he told himself, but how in the world can I get out of it? I can't just sit here and die without even trying to prevent it. What was it that baseball announcer on the radio back home used to say all the time? "The game isn't over until the last ball has been pitched." He looked around. Were there any more balls to be pitched? It didn't look like it.

All right, then, *was* there anything at all he could try? The thing that had him trapped was a few feet of icy water. He could swim. No matter what the hazards might be down there in the flooded tunnel before him, swimming gave him a lot more chance of coming out alive than just standing here worrying while he slowly froze to death. No, sir, maybe the last ball hasn't been pitched yet.

Jerry reached over and put an arm around the boy's shoulder. "Look, Joe," he said, "there's only one way we can get out of here and that's by swimming under water. Now I don't think we're very far from the opening and we shouldn't have to swim more than a few feet, so get on my back and when I say the word take a deep breath and hold it and don't let go of me, no matter what happens."

The boy stood looking toward the place where the tunnel roof sloped down to meet the surface of the black, sinister water. "I'm scared," he said, starting to cry again.

"It's the only chance we've got, Joe," Jerry said sternly. "Get on my back. Hurry!"

They put the lanterns down. Joe climbed onto his back and Jerry started wading. Each step took him deeper into the water, so cold it seemed to burn before it numbed him. First his knees, then his thighs, and when the water level was almost to his hips Joe let go and scrambled back into the tunnel. "I ain't goin'!" he cried in a panicky voice.

Jerry turned back and held a hand out to the boy. "Come on, Joe, there's nothing to it. One deep breath and we'll be out. It can't be more than ten feet and I've swum under water lots of times. Come on!"

Joe ran further back into the tunnel as Jerry came toward him. "I won't do it," he shouted. "I'm scared of the water."

"You're liable to die in here if you don't try it."

"I'd rather be dead than go in the water!"

Jerry realized he was wasting his time trying to argue with the frightened boy, so he decided to go it alone. If he got out somehow he might be able to save Joe. If he stayed here they wouldn't have a chance.

Instead of wading forward slowly to where the roof sloped down into the water and ducking under, Jerry went back into the mine about fifty feet, turned and ran down the incline as fast as he could and flung himself forward and downward into the water with a powerful running dive. As he swam down the flooded tunnel he felt as though he was making a one-way trip through a water main. No turning back now and there was no coming up to fill his aching lungs with air. He had been under water only a few seconds when he started to see bright flashes before his eyes. The cold stiffened his muscles and made them want to cramp.

When he thought he could hold his breath no longer, Jerry was abruptly sucked out of the tunnel by the current racing past. He changed the angle of his body and making one last effort fought his way upward. The next instant he was at the surface, gulping in lungsful of the sweet open air, unmindful of the muddy torrent that bore him along. 100, 200, 300 yards he was carried before his strength returned and he could swim toward the bank.

Pulling himself out of the water, he sat for a few minutes shivering and gasping for breath. The cold was intense.

When he had his wind back Jerry left the stream and headed for the tents. "Oh, there you are," Mrs. Kashook said. "I been callin' you boys for dinner half an hour. You look like you fell in. Where's Joe?"

Jerry looked down for a moment then said, "He's—Joe's still in the tunnel."

"Why didn't he come back with you?"

"Look, Mrs. Kashook," Jerry said, "there's nothing to worry about. Joe's all right. But while we were inside the old Russian mine Gus Kramer's dam washed away and the water trapped us. I tried to get him to come with me when I swam out but he wouldn't do it."

"Where's that tunnel?" the Indian woman asked.

"I'll show you." Jerry led the way to the creek and pointed to the place beneath the swirling water.

Jerry shuddered as he looked down into the murky water. He had swum in that stream once already and had had enough of it. Even if there had been the possibility of somehow swimming back into the tunnel for Joe he knew he wouldn't have done it. Glacier Creek was too much for him. But how then *could* they get the boy out? The only thing he could think of was to lower the water again, to dam the stream once more. "Go find a shovel," he said to Mrs. Kashook. He hurried to the flume and got the shovel he had been using.

Anna Kashook ran to the diggings over on the No. 4 claim and came back with another shovel. Standing high on the bank above the narrow bend where the ditch entered the creek, they began shoveling gravel down into the water as fast as they could. After ten minutes of frantic work Jerry stopped and said, "It's no use, Mrs. Kashook. The water is washing the gravel away as fast as we throw it in. We're just wasting our time."

Joe's mother shook her head and tossed the coarse, black hair out of her eyes. "We got to do somethin'," she said, pitching more gravel into the stream. "Got to get my little boy out."

"The only thing that will move the dirt fast enough to stop all that water is Gus's—Uncle Ed's bulldozer."

Jerry threw his shovel down. "I'm going to get it." Untying one of the horses he climbed on bareback and headed for the lake. As he neared the thickets that covered the last quarter mile the horse suddenly snorted, whirled about and refused to go on. It pawed the ground nervously and looked with wild eyes off into the saplings. Jerry knew the horse had scented the odor of the dead bear and would go no further. He would have to go the rest of the way on foot.

Jerry followed the tread marks into the thicket where his uncle had hidden the tractor. Climbing up onto the big, yellow machine he unscrewed the cap from the fuel tank and looked in. There was some oil in the bottom, possibly enough to get him back up to the glacier, but not enough, he thought, to do the bulldozing necessary to block the stream off. Gus's boat was still lying on the beach, laden with barrels of diesel oil. No one but Gus himself should complain if he took just enough to do the job he had to do. He would borrow what he needed and Ed could pay it back when he returned from Seward.

He experimented with different combinations of levers, switches and buttons, until the engine finally started. It ran roughly at first, then settled down to a steady throb as Jerry figured out what the various controls were used for. He always had had a knack for machinery and was thankful for it now.

He disengaged the clutch, put the gearshift into the position he thought reverse would be, then slowly let the clutch out. As the tractor began to move backwards, he opened the throttle a bit, let the clutch completely out and began trying out the two steering levers. He stopped the machine, put it into a forward gear and headed for the lake, feeling quite pleased with himself.

By the time he reached the beach Jerry had a pretty good idea of how the tractor operated. He pulled up beside the yellow shovelnose and, leaving the engine idling, filled the fuel tank from one of Gus's barrels. Then he started back for the glacier. He would have liked to have driven the tractor at full speed but the way ahead was rocky and the ground uneven so he drove along at half throttle.

Anna Kashook was still shoveling gravel into the stream when Jerry got there. He waved her aside and drove up onto the ridge that divided the No. 3 and No. 4 claims. Putting the tractor into first gear he lowered the bulldozer blade and began shoving great heaps of dirt into the creek. At first the current carried the gravel off downstream but gradually he began to gain on it. Finally the flow stopped and the water level below the fill began to drop. A few minutes later the tunnel opening appeared in the canyon wall. Like a timid rabbit, Joe Kashook stuck his head out, looked around cautiously, then jumped out of the mine and ran down the empty stream bed as though the ghosts of the dead men within were after him.

A great weight seemed to lift from Jerry as he saw the frightened boy go to his mother's arms.

## CHAPTER XV

Late the next afternoon Jerry took Joe and his mother with him when he drove the tractor back to the beach to meet his uncle and Mike Kashook. "Well, well," Ed said when the two boats, heavily loaded with drums of diesel oil, had landed, "I didn't know you could handle a cat."

"Neither did I," Jerry said, "until I had to."

"Had to?"

Instead of answering, Jerry reached into his pocket and took out the piece of quartz he had found in the mine tunnel. "Here's a funny looking rock I picked up yesterday," he said, feigning ignorance. "Do you know what it is?"

Ed took the specimen of ore and examined it. He opened his knife and dug out one of the larger specks of yellow metal. He laid it on a rock and hit it with another, then picked up the flattened nugget and scratched it with his knife blade. "Jerry," he said, with excitement in his voice, "just where did you get this?"

"I found it on the No. 3 claim. Why?"

"Why? It so happens that this passes all the tests for high grade gold. Where on the claim did you find it?"

"I'd have to show you. Does it have much gold in it?"

"It will have to be assayed to tell just how good it really is." Ed hefted the quartz in his hand. "But I'd say if we can just find the vein it came out of we'll have it made."

"Well," Jerry said, grinning, "that's just where I found it—in the vein."

"You aren't kidding me, are you?"

"Cross my heart, hope to die," Jerry said. "We found the vein, all right. Or, rather, Joe saw the tunnel first."

"Vein—tunnel?"

Jerry went over the events of the previous day quickly. "Jerry, lad," his uncle said when he had finished, "I don't like all these close calls you've been having and it's my fault for going off and leaving you alone before you've learned how to take care of yourself."

"I always have been lucky," Jerry said.

"But you can't depend on your luck to hold forever. I'm going to keep you under my wing from now on, at least until you've learned what to be scared of. Now let's get up to that old Russian mine and see whether or not you've made your fortune."

"Made my fortune?"

"Sure! Didn't I tell you you'd get a share of everything we took out of the ground?"

"But—"

"No 'buts' about it. In this business we share and share alike." Then he added, "And wait until Anvil hears about this. He'll get well in a hurry when he finds out we've hit the mother lode—if it is the mother lode, and I'll bet it is."

"I wonder how Anvil is?" Jerry said.

"We stopped at Kenai and saw him on the way back from Seward. He's got so many bandages on he looks like a mummy, but it's all they can do to keep him in bed, in spite of his broken leg."

"I'm sure glad to hear that."

"All right," Ed said, "everybody up on the cat! All aboard for the millionaire's special!"

"How about the oil?" Mike asked, indicating the steel drums in the boats.

"That can wait," Jerry's uncle said exuberantly. "All we care about now is that we have enough to get us to the glacier." He pointed to the tractor seat. "Start her up." When Jerry had the engine running he said, "Home, James, and don't spare the horses!"

When they reached the No. 3 claim, Jerry stopped at the edge of the stream bed opposite the door of the tunnel. Without getting off the tractor Ed looked down into the dark entrance for a time then said, "I'd have never believed it! And we've got Gus Kramer to thank for this, too. If he hadn't dammed up the ditch the creek bed wouldn't have gone dry and we probably never would have found the place." He pointed toward the hole. "Why, I can see the quartz vein from here. Yes, sir, Jerry, it looks like we've struck it all right and as far as I'm concerned our good friend Gus can have the No. 4 and everything beyond it. How far in did you say that tunnel goes?"

"Oh, about 200 or 300 feet. Something like that."

Ed looked up at the row of cairns that stood along the top of the cliff. "200 feet. That's well beyond my east boundary so the first thing we've got to do is go up there and stake out a lode claim so we'll be protected." He looked back toward the tunnel. "But before we do anything else I've got to see the inside of that mine!" Ed got off the tractor and walked up to look at the dam Jerry had built the day before. "I wouldn't go in there for all the gold in the world," he said. "Not until that fill has been reinforced. Do you want to do it or shall I?"

"I can do it," Jerry said. He put the tractor into gear and lowered the 'dozer blade.

"Fine. Add about another twenty-five feet on the upstream side, build it up as high as the top of the bank all the way across to the canyon wall then drive back and forth across her a few times so she'll be packed down good and solid."

When Jerry had finished strengthening the dam his uncle said, "Good job. If that doesn't hold her nothing will. Come on. Let's go have a look in that tunnel."

Carrying a can of kerosene to refill the lanterns he and Joe had left in the mine, Jerry led the way for his uncle and Mike Kashook as they walked up the steep-walled stream bed. "Here it is," he said when they reached the portal, "but I'd like to know why they didn't start digging level with the bottom of the creek instead of four feet up there in the cliff."

"Well," Ed said, "when they started the hole that's probably where the bedrock was. The glacier has ground the rock down that much."

Jerry shook his head in amazement. "You wouldn't

think ice could do that, dig down into four feet of solid rock."

"A glacier is the most powerful bulldozer in the world, when you consider the weight of the thing and the length of time it has to do its work." Ed stepped back and looked at the spot where the strip of quartz disappeared into the opposite wall of the stream bed. "I'd like to know just how far west that vein goes—and how deep." He turned and put his hands on the floor of the tunnel. "Give me a boost, somebody. I can't stand the suspense any longer."

When they were all inside Mike refilled and lighted the lanterns and they started up the tunnel, bending forward to avoid the low ceiling. "I don't see why they didn't make this thing a foot or so higher while they were at it," Jerry complained after hitting his head on a projecting point of rock.

"If you had ever done any hand drilling in hard rock you'd know why," Ed said. "They made this drift just high enough to get to the top of the vein and wide enough to—" He broke off suddenly as they came upon the three bodies lying on the floor at the end of the mine. He looked at each one and then at the powder keg. "Explosion," he said to Jerry.

"How can you tell that?" the boy asked.

"Because both ends are blown out of that powder keg and it's charred inside." Ed pointed toward the two bodies nearest the forward wall. "Those two were double-jacking," he said, "that is, the big fellow with the black whiskers was swinging the hammer and the other one was holding the drill. Look at the face of that bit—it's all burred. When a piece of iron gets that way sparks will fly every time you hit it a good whack with a hammer. Just offhand, I'd say they left their powder keg too close, a spark flew into it and Boom!"

"Wouldn't an explosion burn them or something? They look as though they just lay down there and went to sleep."

"The black powder they used a hundred or so years ago didn't have the force behind it that our explosives have. What probably happened was the concussion knocked them out, the explosion burned all the oxygen out of the air and they suffocated before they had a chance to come to." Ed nodded toward the third body beside the wooden box on runners. "This old fellow must have been the mule—he dragged the ore and rock out of the tunnel."

Jerry called his uncle's attention to the chains on their legs.

"Well, that settles something I've wondered about for a good many years," Ed said. "The Russians were supposed to have used prisoners back in the old days to do the hard work and I guess this proves it. An old-timer told me he once found a skeleton in the woods with a chain on the leg bones but I never really believed him. I guess he was telling the truth after all."

Ed reached into the box and took out a chunk of quartz. "Well, boys, we've got our work cut out for us, but it's going to take a lot of equipment to do this thing the way it should be done. We're going to have to have an air compressor to run the jackhammers and for ventilation. We'll need a power plant for lights, a lot of wire, pipe and plenty of dynamite. Then we'll need track and some cars to get the ore out, and we'll have to set up a stamp mill to separate the gold from the quartz. On top of it all we'll have to bring everything in by tractor train this winter after the freeze-up. And it's going to take a lot of sweat and hard work."

"Won't it take a lot of money, too?" Jerry asked.

"You bet it will take money and that's something we don't have much of."

"Where will we get it?"

Jerry's uncle thought for a moment. "As I see it we're going to have to go full blast at placer mining for the rest of the season. Now that we've got the bulldozer, we can work a lot more gravel between now and the time snow flies than we'd ever do with a pick and shovel. We'll start right up as close to the vein as we can, and if our luck holds we can take out enough free gold to get us in shape so we can start working the lode next year. That's where the big money will be, in this tunnel, if that ore is as rich as I hope it is."

"What about those dead men?"

"We're going to get them out of here and bury them. After that's done we'd better tear out the fill, and flood the tunnel mouth again. We won't be able to work it until we get equipment in here and the fewer people who know about it the better off we're going to be. Just offhand I'd say—"

Ed was interrupted by a hallooing sound that came from the portal of the mine. They listened and the call came again, "Hey, Mr. Carlson!"

"That's Joe," Mike Kashook said. "I'll go down and see what he wants." He headed toward the tunnel entrance. Jerry's uncle went on talking, explaining the methods they would use to drill and blast the ore out of the mountain. "No double-jacking and black powder for us, Jerry. All my life I've been looking for a decent strike and now that we've got it we're going to do everything right."

In a few minutes the bobbing yellow light of Mike Kashook's lantern appeared again, growing brighter as he returned from the open end of the mine. "You better come on out, Ed," he said.

"What's up?"

"There's a couple of guys out there want to see you."

"Do you know who they are?"

"One of them's that deputy who was down here yesterday."

"What does he want, or did he say?"

"He said it was somethin' to do about you stealin' a cat."

The newcomers were down on their knees on the bedrock examining the quartz vein when Jerry and his companions came out of the tunnel. "Hello, Carlson," the deputy marshal said as he stood up. "It looks like you've got something here."

"Hello, Marshal," Jerry's uncle said, stepping down from the tunnel into the stream bed. "I understand you want to see me about my bulldozer?"

"Why, yes," the officer began. "When I was down here yesterday I thought it looked like one that was reported stolen during the winter. Where did you get it?"

"I bought it, of course."

"Oh, no, you didn't buy it." The second man got quickly to his feet. Jerry looked toward the ruddy-faced and heavily-built man. "That cat was stolen from my lot down on the Sterling Highway during the winter along with about twenty barrels of diesel oil."

"Just who are you anyway, Mister?" Ed asked, narrowing his eyes as he looked at the other man.

"Bill Sweeney, road-building contractor."

"Aren't you the fellow Gus Kramer usually works for?"

"I know Kramer."

"And he's worked for you?"

"He's worked for me, yes. What of it? A lot of people have worked for me."

"I bought the machine from him," Ed said.

"Can you prove it?"

"Sure, I can prove it," Ed said. "I've got a bill of sale—that should be proof enough."

The contractor snorted. "Anyone can write out a bill of sale. Anybody who'd steal a tractor wouldn't stop at forging a piece of paper to cover it up."

"I was there when he bought it," Mike Kashook spoke up.

Bill Sweeney turned and gave the Indian a hard, piercing look. "I don't believe I was talking to you."

"But me and my wife signed the paper," Mike persisted.

"And I saw them do it," Jerry added.

"Where I come from," the contractor said, sarcastically, "no Siwash's signature is worth the paper it's written on."

"Maybe you better go back where you came from then," Ed said.

Bill Sweeney turned to the deputy. "I swore out a John Doe warrant for the guy who stole my cat. Carlson, here, has it in his possession and claims it's his. So as far as I'm concerned he's John Doe. Serve the warrant on him, Marshal."

"Let's not be in a hurry, Bill," the deputy said. "You don't want to leave yourself open for a false-arrest suit, do you? Maybe we'd better look at the bill of sale first."

"I don't think there ever was any bill of sale."

"There sure was," Jerry said, angrily. His uncle looked at him, frowned and shook his head. Jerry said no more but it was hard to remain silent under the circumstances.

"Do you have it, Carlson?" the deputy asked.

"Sure, I have it."

"Could I see it?"

Ed felt through his clothes. "I know I put it in one of my pockets when Gus gave it to me. Do you remember what I had on, Jerry?"

"Your brown jacket, wasn't it?" Jerry said.

"Let's see now, where did I put that brown jacket?"

"Say, Ed," Mike Kashook said, "didn't you take it off when we were loading the oil barrels onto the truck over at Seward?"

"By golly, that's just what I did," Ed said. "And I

hung it on the side of a boxcar on that freight train that was standing on the railroad tracks there alongside the dock. It's probably somewhere between Seward and Fairbanks by now, if it didn't blow off along the line."

The contractor snorted again. "I've heard everything! As far as I'm concerned this is the bird we're looking for, Marshal. If he isn't I'll take the consequences."

"Well, Carlson," the officer was taking a piece of paper from his pocket, "I guess I'll have to serve this warrant on you and take you in." He handed over the paper, and took out a pair of handcuffs. "I'm sorry but I guess I'll have to put these on you."

"You don't need to put bracelets on me," Jerry's uncle protested. "I won't try to get away."

The marshal shook his head. "Sorry, but you're charged with a felony so I've got to put them on you. Would you hold out your hands, please?"

Ed put his hands out and the marshal snapped the handcuffs on. "This part of it I don't like," Ed said, "but I guess there's a first time for everything."

"Where are you going to take him?" Jerry asked in a troubled voice.

"To Anchorage," the marshal answered.

"Don't you worry any," Jerry's uncle said. "I'll get this thing straightened out and be back tomorrow. You just get busy and do what's got to be done." He looked Jerry straight in the eye. "And do it as quick as you can."

They all left the stream bed and when they reached the helicopter that was waiting near the wanigan Bill

Sweeney said, "There's no way to get that cat out of here until after freeze-up this coming winter, but I'm going to fix it so nobody will be able to use it anyway." He borrowed a wrench from the pilot, and removed a piece of equipment from the side of the engine. "There," he said when he returned, "she'll sit there till Doomsday without a fuel injector."

The marshal reached out and took the injector from the contractor. "I'll have to take that, Bill," he said, "since the machine is under the jurisdiction of the Justice Department now."

"Everybody ready to go?" the pilot asked as he prepared to start the helicopter.

"Where do you want to go, Bill?" the marshal asked.

"You can take me back to Kenai," the contractor said. "I've got to get back on the job. I'm behind on my schedule as it is, thanks to tractor thieves."

Jerry saw his uncle's jaw muscles tighten and his handcuffed fists clench. "Marshal, if you'll take me over to Seward to see if I can find my jacket and the bill of sale, I'll pay any extra cost that's involved," he said.

"We'll see what we can do, Carlson, but I won't make any promises until we get to Kenai and I can put in a call to Anchorage. My orders are to bring you in and I can't make any side trips without getting an O.K. from the boss first." He strapped Ed into the rear seat and got in beside him. Bill Sweeney settled in the front seat beside the pilot, the door was closed, the rotor began to spin and the helicopter rose into the air and flew off toward the north.

## CHAPTER XVI

Jerry stood for a time watching the helicopter getting smaller in the distance. When it had disappeared he turned to Mike Kashook and said bitterly, "I'll bet Gus was behind this somehow. We know Uncle Ed didn't steal that tractor. Something sure must be rotten up here or Gus couldn't always have the law on his side."

"Some day he'll go too far," Mike said. "Sometime he'll bite off more than he can chew."

"Well, I guess there's nothing *I* can do about it."

"Give a fella like that enough rope and some day he'll hang himself," Mike said.

"Yes, but when?" Jerry's voice was still bitter. "I wonder what Uncle Ed meant when he said to get busy and do what's got to be done?"

"We got to open up the fill, and let the water in the creek again."

"That will be an awful job without the bulldozer."

"Nothin' to it," Mike said. "There's some dynamite in Gus's tent. We'll just shoot a couple of holes in the dam and she'll go out, just like that." He snapped his fingers.

"Oh, yes, and I just remembered that he said lode claims have to be staked out. Maybe that's what he meant."

"That's right. You got to stake 'em to hold 'em."

"How do you stake a claim, anyway, Mike?"

"You got me. I've worked on lots of 'em but I never staked out none."

That, Jerry thought, seemed to be the most important thing to be done—especially since other people knew about the mine and the lode vein now. From here on out it would be a matter of first come, first served. If anyone else came along and staked out the lode it would be theirs. But how was it done, anyway? He recalled the mining book his uncle had referred to in the cabin by the lake. "Say, Mike," he said, "I just remembered Uncle Ed has a book on mining laws and things. I think I'll go down and see if it's got anything in it about staking claims."

"O.K., and I'll get the dynamite planted."

"Fine. What would be the best way to get up there on the cliff?"

"About half a mile this side of the lake, over on the other side of the creek, you just go up through the timber and first thing you know you'll be on top."

"Thanks," Jerry said. "I don't know how long this will take but I'll be back as soon as I can. And for gosh sakes, don't blow up that dam before I get back because I don't feel like taking any more swims in Glacier Creek. Once is enough!"

Back at the cabin by Tustumena Lake, Jerry read the

page in the mining book under the heading, "Location of Lode Claims":

"A location notice must contain the names of the locator or locators, the date of location, and a description of the claim by reference to some natural object or permanent monument that will identify it. . . .

"Lode claims are limited to 1,500 feet in length and 300 feet on each side of the lode or vein at the surface. . . . The end lines of the claim must be parallel. . . ."

Well, he thought, that should be easy enough. He closed the book and put it back on the shelf. He found a pen, and took an empty fruit jar from a cupboard to put his location notice in for protection from the weather. Then he left the cabin and followed the trail to Glacier Creek, walking along the east bank of the stream. It was an hour's stiff climb before he came out of the woods to barren rock, and the top of the canyon wall.

He walked along the rim of the cliff toward the row of cairns that marked the eastern boundary of his uncle's placer claims. He kept on until he reached the third monument, the pile of stones that marked the beginning of the No. 3 claim. The tunnel lay somewhere below him now but he was not sure just exactly where in relation to the third and fourth monuments. He tried to remember what he had read in the book before leaving the cabin and wished he had brought it along. Didn't it say, "300 feet on each side of the vein"? Yes, he was sure of that.

He approached the edge of the cliff cautiously and looked over. Directly ahead and below he could see the tents on the No. 4 claim. A little to the right were the wanigan and the disabled tractor. The picketed horses were searching for stray wisps of hay and Jerry reminded himself that as soon as he got back down there they must be fed. To his left he could see the edge of the glacier. Beyond was the main body of ice, like a great blue-white river that had been frozen in its course.

He could not see the Indian people, but he could hear the sound of their voices and the ring of shovels coming up from below. Edging as close as he dared to the lip of the canyon wall, he lay on his stomach and looked down at the empty stream bed. A little to the left he could see Mike Kashook and his wife and Joe, all busily digging holes into the top of the dam. "Hey, down there!" he called.

All three stopped working and looked up. Mike waved and called back, "Hey, yourself! Made it all right, huh?"

"Nothing to it!" Jerry shouted down. "Would you go and stand in front of the tunnel?"

Mike put his shovel down, left the fill and walked along the stream bed. He stopped a short distance below the flume. "She's right in there!" he yelled, pointing toward the cliff.

"Good!" Jerry marked the spot with a rock. He stood back and looked first at the No. 3 monument then at the No. 4. For all practical purposes the tunnel was almost in the middle of the No. 3 claim so he tore down the No. 3 and No. 4 monuments and re-erected them, each thirty feet closer to the center. Now they conformed with the regulation that a lode claim should be sixty feet narrower than a placer claim. Why the difference, he wondered.

Next he had to pace off 1,500 feet to the east and build two more monuments. Then he must write his name and his uncle's name and the date, with a rough description of the location on a piece of paper, put it in the fruit jar and leave it there.

Jerry began walking and counting his paces. How long were his steps and how many of them would it take to make 1,500 feet? He made two or three trial starts and estimated his paces to be about thirty inches long. Thirty inches into 1,500 feet, what was that? He never had been any good at doing arithmetic in his head so he took out the pencil and paper and figured: 600 steps.

He started walking again. At the end of 100 paces Jerry picked up a small pebble and when he had six pebbles he stopped and built a monument. He then went north 600 feet and had just started to build the next monument when he heard a threshing over his head. A helicopter was settling down at a steep angle, apparently the same machine that had taken his uncle off in handcuffs earlier in the day. What was it doing back here, anyway? Had Ed gotten things straightened out and returned already? He watched while the 'copter disappeared over the edge of the canyon wall, then hurried to finish building the monument.

When that was done Jerry cut across to the center of the claim and piled up some more rocks. He then filled out the claim notice, putting Ed Carlson's name down first, and then his own. He put the paper into the fruit jar and was just covering it with stones when the helicopter roared up and flew off into the north again. When it was out of sight Jerry went to the edge of the cliff and looked over. Down below he saw two men beating up Mike Kashook!

"Hey, what do you guys think you're doing down there?" Jerry shouted. He instinctively reached for the rifle that had almost become a part of him. Then he remembered he had left it standing in a corner of the cabin down at the lake. Of all the times to have forgotten it! Chalk up another error for Nelson. He grabbed up a fist-sized rock and sailed it down at the combatants—Gus Kramer and Bill Sweeney.

Gus looked up, startled, when the rock landed close by and yelled something to his companion. They both ran as Jerry hurled more rocks after them. When they were out of range Bill Sweeney shook his fist and bellowed, "Come on down off your perch, you buzzard, and we'll give you a dose of the same!"

"I'll be down as soon as I can get there!" Jerry shouted. He turned and headed toward the lake, along the top of the canyon wall, as fast as the rough ground and sharp rocks underfoot permitted.

In a straight line it had been not much more than a hundred feet from the top of the cliff to the spot where the fight had occurred, but it took him the better part of two hours to get there, returning the way he had come. When he arrived the intruders were gone. "What was it all about?" Jerry asked angrily when he came down onto the fill where Mike and his wife and Joe were back at work digging blasting holes. The Indian's eyes were blackened, his lips were cut and swollen, and the bruises on his face made him almost unrecognizable.

Mike stopped digging and leaned on his shovel. "Well," he said, "a little while after you hollered down to me, that whirligig landed and Gus and that fella Bill got out. As soon as the machine was gone they began pilin' up new monuments. I told Gus the ground was already staked and he said the law says he can stake out a lode claim on anybody's placer claim if it ain't already been staked for a lode, too."

Jerry clenched his fists and looked at the ground. "Why must that guy *always* be right?"

"I wonder if he can really do that?" Mike asked.

"I'm afraid so," Jerry said. "I remember seeing that in Uncle Ed's mining book this morning when I was looking for the rules on how to stake out a lode claim. He can stake out a lode claim 25 feet on each side of a vein on any placer claim that hasn't been patented—whatever that means. And then what happened?"

"I told them I didn't know nothin' about the law but that I was supposed to keep them off Ed's property. When I started to get my gun to put them off they beat me up."

"What did they do then?"

"Right after you started back here they finished stakin' out the new claim—and that Bill, he says to Gus, 'What about the top of the cliff?' and Gus, he says to Bill, 'The kid's probably staked that for us'."

"I did not stake it for them. Where are they now?"

"Soon as they was done they left here in an awful hurry."

"How did they go?"

"On foot, headin' for the lake."

"Gus's shovelnose is still down there." Jerry thought for a moment. "I'll bet I know what they're going to do, Mike. They're heading for the Land Office so they can file on that vein. If they get there first it will be theirs and there's nothing anybody can do about it."

"I guess they got themselves a claim then," Mike said, resignedly.

"Maybe I can catch them."

Mike shook his head. "They got better than an hour's head start. And besides, you could never catch them anyway. That shovelnose is the fastest boat on the inlet."

Jerry angered. "We can't just sit here and let them steal our mine and not even try to do anything to stop them."

Mike shrugged. "There just ain't nothin' you can do."

"Well, I'm going to do *something."* Jerry tried to think what he *could* do. Here was another case of the game not being over until the last ball was pitched. How could he beat Gus Kramer and Bill Sweeney to the Land Office, or prevent them from getting there? He thought of something. "Say, Mike, isn't Gus's boat still loaded with those barrels of diesel oil he brought up the day Anvil was hurt?"

"It was the last I saw it."

"I don't think he'd leave that oil down there on the

beach—and if he took it with him, I'll bet we'd have a chance to catch up with him after all."

"No, he couldn't make any headway with a load like that." Mike hesitated. "But what'll you do if you do catch him? Those guys'll beat your brains out—if not somethin' worse."

"Oh, no they won't! I'm not going to monkey around." Jerry headed for the wanigan to get Ed's rifle. "This time he's bitten off more than he can chew."

"You better be sure you don't bite off more'n *you* can chew," Mike called after him.

"Don't worry. I can take care of myself!"

They rode the horses bareback to the lake. When they got there the shovelnose was nowhere in sight and the beach was strewn with barrels of oil. "Well, I guess that takes care of that," Jerry said, all the enthusiasm gone from him. He stood for a time looking silently across the water in the direction the yellow shovelnose must have gone. Never in his life had he felt so helpless and frustrated. What can I do now, he wondered. The answer was obvious and too simple—nothing. Any way he looked at it, he was licked. Gus and Bill were probably already at the far end of the lake. They were very likely shooting the rapids of the Kasilof right now. By the time he could get to Slackwater in his uncle's boat they would have reached the lower river and be well on their way to Anchorage. And if he did get to Slackwater, what good would that do? Jerry didn't know if he had the guts to run the river again. Sure, he'd done it when Anvil's life had been at stake.

And he'd wrecked a boat in the process. Was ownership of the mine worth the risk a second time?

Mike Kashook's voice broke into his thoughts. "What are you goin' to do now, Jerry?"

Jerry looked about at the mountains and the forest. He went quickly over all the angles again, weighed the possibilities against the risks. As far as he was concerned more than money was at stake. He knew there was a principle involved but he couldn't quite put his finger on it.

"Whatcha goin' to do?" Mike repeated.

Jerry headed for the water's edge. "I'm going to shoot the works, Mike. Let's unload Uncle Ed's boat so I can get going."

They got busy and unloaded the heavy barrels of diesel oil from the white boat. When the job was done Mike suggested maybe he should go along.

"No," Jerry said, putting the rifle into the boat, "I think you'd better go back to the claim and keep an eye on things."

"You be careful," the Indian said. "Those guys won't stop at nothin'."

"Shove me out," Jerry shouted.

Mike shoved the boat out into the lake. Jerry lowered the motors over the stern and pulled on the starting handles of first one and then the other. "They won't go!" he yelled.

"Look in the gas tanks!" the Indian shouted back. "Maybe they drained them before they left!"

Both tanks were empty. "How about your boat, Mike? Do you have any gas?"

Mike looked. "None in mine, either!"

"I'll row down to the cabin and get some more!"

"O.K., I'll run down and have it ready when you get there!" The Indian waded across the now shallow mouth of Glacier Creek and headed at a trot for Ed's cabin. It took nearly half an hour of hard, impatient rowing to get the heavy boat to where Mike was waiting on the shore with several five-gallon cans of gasoline. They lost no time filling the tanks of the outboard motors, and then Jerry shot off for Slackwater.

When he was about halfway down the lake a sudden gust of wind struck him on the back of the neck. A williwaw had sprung up off Tustumena Glacier and a line of whitecaps was already within a quarter of a mile.

With that first breath of biting wind Jerry recalled Ed's warning about being caught in such a blow. "Run for shelter!" He turned the boat to the left, away from the westerly course he had been following, and headed for the protection of a wooded point of land to the south. He had hardly gotten lined up on the new bearing when the full force of the williwaw was upon him. Surrounded by seas that slapped viciously against the side of the dory, breaking inboard and drenching him with an icy spray, Jerry feared the boat would capsize. He swung it about so as to quarter into the rising, steep-sided swells, then eased off on the throttles. With reduced power and the new heading, the boat rode easier despite the violent wind that howled in his ears and soaked him time and again with sheets of bitterly cold water.

He was still a hundred yards away from the point of land when a great combing sea came rolling down the lake. Already several inches deep with sloshing water, the boat would not lift before the comber and it broke inboard. When it had passed on, the motors were dead, he was without control and the hull was half full of water. He grabbed the oars, put them in place and held the sodden, sluggish craft bow to the wind as best he could. A fine, smoke-like haze of driving moisture obscured the distant mountains and made the nearby land appear but a shadow in the mist.

He found that the wind was not entirely his enemy but was actually helping him a little. Each gust nudged him a bit closer to shore and after what seemed to be an eternity he was almost in behind the shelter of the trees that grew upon the point. He put his weight to the oars but when he was still a hundred feet from shore another big comber swept inboard, the boat swamped and he found himself swimming. "Nelson sinks another boat!" he cried aloud as he struck out for the shore. "Three in one week—not bad! If I keep this up there won't be a boat left afloat in Alaska!"

Halfway to shore he felt solid ground beneath him and waded the rest of the way.

## CHAPTER XVII

Marooned!

Jerry Nelson might as well have been cast away upon a desert island as stranded here on the south shore of Tustumena Lake without his rifle and without even a knife to defend himself. "Well, I asked for it," he told himself as he got in behind a tree and took off his clothes to wring them out. "I shot the works and look at me now!" He shivered as he got back into his damp garments. "What do I do next?"

He wondered just exactly where he was but thought he was quite a bit closer to the lower end of the lake than he was to the glacier. He didn't have a chance in the world now of getting to the Land Office before Gus Kramer did. But he couldn't stay here. He began walking to the westward, stopping now and then to eat the sweet, yellow salmonberries that grew here and there on bushes close to the water's edge. He was starving—and wished that he'd taken time to have a meal before he'd left the diggings.

Billowing masses of black rain clouds were passing overhead. They made Jerry feel this was not just a local williwaw that would shortly die away but, rather, a storm of major proportions blowing in from the Pacific Ocean that lay just beyond the Kenai Mountains to the east.

Time and again as he walked along the strip of narrow beach, breakers surged up and almost dragged him back into the lake. But he dared not go further inland for fear of meeting another brownie. The forest was much too close.

Hour upon hour Jerry struggled down the wave-swept beach, soaked over and over again, by the driving rain and spray. He wanted to find a place of shelter where he could rest and warm himself. But there was no shelter and he could only keep moving. If he stopped, he felt he might never go on again.

Jerry had the feeling that had he somehow been transported back through time to the days of the Gold Rush, he would have been no worse off than he actually was. He could understand now why Anvil Bergen had no desire to return to the old days when men had had to walk wherever they went and carried their possessions on their backs. He was thankful he had nothing to carry.

Born in the gasoline age, Jerry wasn't accustomed to walking great distances. But now that the chips were down, it was either walk or stay put. He found he *could* do it. But he wasn't enjoying it a bit. He tried not to think of hiking the ten miles or so to Slackwater and beyond. Instead, he walked just to the next tree and then went on to the wave-washed boulder ahead. From there he made it to a clump of bushes that lay beyond, and so on and on. Again he heard Anvil's voice, ". . . walking, walking, walking—always walking."

To take his mind off himself and the problems ahead he started thinking about things back home; his folks and his friends. And what about Russ Wheeler? He wondered how *he* would hold up under the circumstances of the present moment. Jerry had been drawn to Russ, admired him, and even feared him just a bit because he was a tough guy, a fellow who'd spit in the eye of the devil himself and wasn't afraid to shoot his mouth off to anybody. But did a loud mouth and contempt for the law indicate toughness? Or was it, rather, a sign of rudeness and ignorance?

A week ago Jerry would have pitted Russ against anyone. But now—well, he didn't know for sure. What would Russ do if *he* were set down here like this? What would Russ have done had it been up to *him* to kill the brownie? Or run Silver Salmon Rapids to get Anvil to the doctor? He had no way of knowing what Russ would have done but he did know what he himself had done. The very thought of his accomplishments put fresh strength into his tired legs.

At last he saw ahead the narrow opening that marked the entrance to Slackwater. Here in the lee of a timbered peninsula the storm was less severe, and in a short while Jerry found himself on the bank of the channel. His heart leaped. At last his luck was beginning to turn. A short distance away was a cabin. There was smoke blowing from the chimney. But it was on the opposite bank.

He went on until he was directly across the channel

from the cabin. He cupped his hands and called out, "Hey!" The wind snatched the cry away. He called again, louder, but there was still no sign that anyone had heard. Jerry called again and again but no one came to the door. He began to wonder if there was anyone there at all. There must be, though. Besides the smoke coming from the chimney, a dory with outboard motor on the stern was drawn up half out of the water and tied to a tree. Out here wherever a man's boat was, he had to be there, too.

One thing sure—if he didn't find somebody soon he'd have to go on, or else swim Slackwater. And that idea he didn't like at all. No, he'd rather keep walking than take any more swims. He waited a few minutes and when a brief lull came in the wind he cupped his hands and called again, "Hey, over there!"

An instant later the cabin door opened and a tall, lean man with a dark mustache looked out. He turned his head this way and that as though trying to hear. Jerry called again and waved. The man saw him then, and came down the bank. He pushed his boat out into the water and rowed across the narrow channel.

Jerry didn't wait for an invitation but climbed into the boat the instant it touched shore. His rescuer rowed him back to the other side. "You look about froze," he said when he had the boat tied to the tree again. "Come on up to the shack and get thawed out."

The cabin was small and cluttered, but never in his life had anything felt so good as the warmth of the little hut. "You'd better get out of those wet duds and into my bunk," the man said. He reached for the coffee pot that simmered on the back of the iron stove.

Out of his clothes and wrapped in the bearskin that covered the bunk, Jerry sipped a cup of hot, black coffee and looked at the world with a new outlook. When he finally stopped shivering he said to his host, "I'll bet you're wondering how I got here."

"You bet I am. What are you doing so far from home, Jerry Nelson?"

Jerry startled. "How do you know who I am?"

The man grinned. "Your dad's name is Erik and your mother is Hilda. You're Ed Carlson's nephew."

"Oh, you've been talking to Uncle Ed, I'll bet."

"Not since last fall, I haven't."

"Then how do you know so much about me? Who are you, anyway?"

"A few winters ago I got crippled up by a crazy moose and went Outside to get patched up and—"

"You're Cliff Steele!"

"Right."

"You've grown a mustache since I last saw you. No wonder I didn't recognize you." They shook hands.

"You've done some growing yourself," Cliff said. A serious look came over his face. "But what's happened, Jerry? Are you in some kind of trouble?"

Jerry went quickly over the circumstances that had brought him here. When he finished Cliff said, "I saw that yellow shovelnose go by here not long before the williwaw struck. They're probably in Anchorage by now."

"Well, there goes the mine!"

"So what?" Steele said. "It's only money."

"Only money," Jerry agreed. "I think that's just exactly the way dad would look at it, too."

Late in the afternoon the wind died and when Tustumena had calmed, Cliff Steele took Jerry back to the upper end of the lake in his boat. Just before they reached the landing near the mouth of Glacier Creek a float plane flew out of the north, circled and landed. It taxied to the beach, and a figure jumped ashore. Then the airplane took off again. Ed Carlson was standing at the water's edge when the dory grounded. The handcuffs were no longer on his wrists. Jerry jumped ashore and decided to beat his uncle to the punch. "I suppose you're wondering what's happened to your boat," he said.

Ed looked around the beach. "Why, I didn't even notice it was gone."

"Well, I sank it."

"How?"

"I got caught out in a williwaw and didn't quite make it to shelter when she swamped."

"Oh, well, we can always build a new one."

Ed's manner surprised Jerry. He had expected to get a first rate bawling-out. "I lost the motors, too, and your best gun went down with the boat."

"Maybe we can salvage them when the water level drops this fall."

Since he'd apparently caught his uncle in a good mood, Jerry decided to jump in with both feet and get all the bad news over with. "I guess it's my fault we lost the mine, too."

"What makes you think we've lost the mine?"

Jerry told him about Gus Kramer and Bill Sweeney returning to the claim. "That's how I happened to be out on the lake when the williwaw struck—I was trying to catch up with them so they wouldn't file on the lode claim before we could do it."

"It's just as well you didn't catch up with them. They're both pretty tough customers."

"For gosh sakes," Jerry flared, "you sound like you don't care whether you lose the mine or not."

"Is that what's bothering you?"

"Isn't that enough?"

Ed threw back his head and laughed until Jerry thought he'd lost his senses. "What's funny?" he asked.

Ed got control of himself. "Well, Jerry, it looks like Gus has outsmarted himself again."

"I don't get it."

"If he and Bill Sweeney hadn't rigged that tractor-stealing deal against me the marshal wouldn't have taken me to Anchorage and I probably wouldn't have beaten them to the Land Office."

Jerry's heart leaped. "Then we didn't lose the mine after all?"

"Why, no, of course not. I went to the Land Office the minute we hit Anchorage. Did you get the claim staked out?"

"I sure did."

"Then we've got her sewed up."

Jerry felt like turning a cartwheel but settled for a quick jig. "Oh boy, oh boy, oh boy! Is Gus going to be surprised when he gets there!"

"Yes, he's probably on the biggest wild goose chase of his career." A serious expression came to Ed's face. "But I've still got that tractor-stealing charge hanging over my head. The only reason I'm not in jail right now is because a friend put up bail for me."

"Didn't you get that straightened out, too?"

Ed shook his head. "I'm going to have a hard time proving I didn't steal the cat and that's what has me worried."

"Wouldn't they let you go to Seward to see if you could find the bill of sale?"

"Oh, we went to Seward, all right, but the boxcar I'd hung my jacket on was gone."

Jerry angered. "Bill of sale or no bill of sale, we know you didn't steal that cat!"

"Sure, we know it but it's going to take a long time to prove it without some good solid evidence in my favor."

Cliff Steele had been standing by listening. He scratched his head and frowned. "What's all this business about a tractor, anyway, Ed?" he asked.

Ed told him.

"Hmmm," Cliff said. "Is that cat painted yellow?"

"Yes."

"And does it have a 'dozer blade on front and a winch on the back?"

"Yes, why?"

"Well, one day back about the middle of February when I was out working my trapline between here and the Caribou Hills I stood in a clump of willows at the edge of a frozen swamp and watched a yellow cat go by dragging a sled loaded with oil barrels. At the time I figured it was hauling stuff in for some of these petroleum geologists, so I didn't think any more about it."

"Did you get a look at the driver?"

"Sure. It was Gus Kramer. He had another fellow with him, too."

"Did you recognize him?"

"I never saw the guy before or since."

"What did he look like?"

"He was so bundled up in his parka I didn't get a very good look at him, but I'd say he was a little taller than Gus and a few years older. Kind of red-faced."

"That would be Bill Sweeney," Ed said. "Would you be willing to go to Anchorage with me and give an affidavit about what you've just told me?"

"You bet I would."

"That might be just the evidence I need to get this thing straightened out," Ed said. The frown left his face and he smiled again.

"But why would they accuse you of stealing it," Jerry asked, "if it wasn't even stolen at all?"

"There might be any number of reasons. When I was up at Anchorage with the marshal I heard rumors that before Sweeney's cat was 'stolen,' he was a long way behind on his payments."

"Then he stole it himself from the guy he owed the money to?"

"That's just an assumption—maybe he didn't. The real reason could have been to get me out of the way."

"Can't you have them put in jail or sue them for false arrest or something like that?" Jerry asked.

"Oh, I suppose I could," Ed said, "but we've got the mine and as long as I get my name cleared that's all I want out of it." He turned to Steele. "What do you say we head for Anchorage, Cliff, and get that affidavit taken care of?"

"I'm ready any time you are."

Ed turned to Jerry. "Do you want to take a trip to the city with us?"

"Well—"

"We just might have a little excitement up there if we should run into Gus and Bill," his uncle added. "And that's a promise."

"Nothing doing," Jerry said. "I've had enough excitement in the past week to last me for a long time. I think I'll go up to the claim and do some nice, quiet work with the muck stick."

"Suit yourself," Ed smiled. "But you're welcome to come along if you want to."

"No, I think I'd better stay here where I can keep out of trouble for a change."

Cliff filled his gas tank and the two men shoved off. Jerry stood on the shore looking after them for a time. He never thought he'd see the day when he'd stay out in the wilderness in preference to a trip to town. This kind of life was beginning to grow on him and he was starting to understand how people could give up the things to be had in the city to live out in the back country.

When the boat was a tiny speck vanishing down the

lake, he left the beach and headed for the trail that lay between the thickets and Glacier Creek. The stream was running bankful again, swift and muddy. Mike Kashook must have blasted out the dam.

He heard a rustling in the underbrush off to his right. At the sound, the hair raised up on the back of his neck and his heart began to pound. It wasn't far from here that Anvil Bergen had met the brownie. Jerry stopped in his tracks and stood quivering as he looked about, trying to locate and identify the sound. What could he do if it was a bear? The creek wasn't far away. He could always go for another swim. He hoped bears didn't like water.

The rustling of leaves came again, followed by a low, bleating sound, then a trembling, long-legged moose calf came wobbling out of the bushes.

"Whew, am I glad to see you!" Jerry said. The calf took a few more stumbling steps, lost its footing and fell down. Jerry hurried over to where it lay panting on the ground. He reached out and it nuzzled his hand with its oversized nose. It showed no fear of him at all and when he rubbed its velvety muzzle it tried to nibble at his fingers. "You act like you're hungry, little fellow," he said. "Where's your mother?"

The calf bleated.

Jerry looked around and listened. He saw and heard nothing.

"Oh, well, you probably know how to take care of yourself." He started to walk away. The calf got to its feet and followed him. Jerry stopped. "Gosh, maybe you're an orphan. I guess I can't leave you here to starve. And besides, the bears or coyotes might get you." The calf nuzzled at his pants leg. "You *are* hungry, aren't you?" He looked down at the calf for a moment and then picked it up in his arms. "You're sure not very heavy. I think I'd better take you up to the claim. Anna Kashook ought to know what to do."

Jerry had taken no more than half a dozen steps when a loud snort came from the thickets. There was a crackling of bushes and a cow moose came charging out into the open. She stood for a moment looking about, sniffing. Then the hairs on her shoulder bristled, her ears lay back against her neck and she came toward Jerry at a dead run. He dropped the calf and scooted up the nearest sapling.

"Now look at me!" Jerry howled angrily as he clung to the uppermost branches of the thin, swaying tree while the moose pawed the ground and snorted beneath him. "I'm the guy who was going to stay here so I could keep out of trouble!"

Suddenly realizing how silly he must look he began to chuckle. "No, sir," he said as he took another grip on the tree trunk, "I can't win. If I don't go hunting for trouble, it comes looking for me."

He resigned himself to an uncomfortable wait but hoped it wouldn't be too long until the moose decided to quit playing games and go off to feed her hungry baby.